Groovy Girls™
Sleep Over Club

Sleepover Surprise
A Twin-sational Birthday

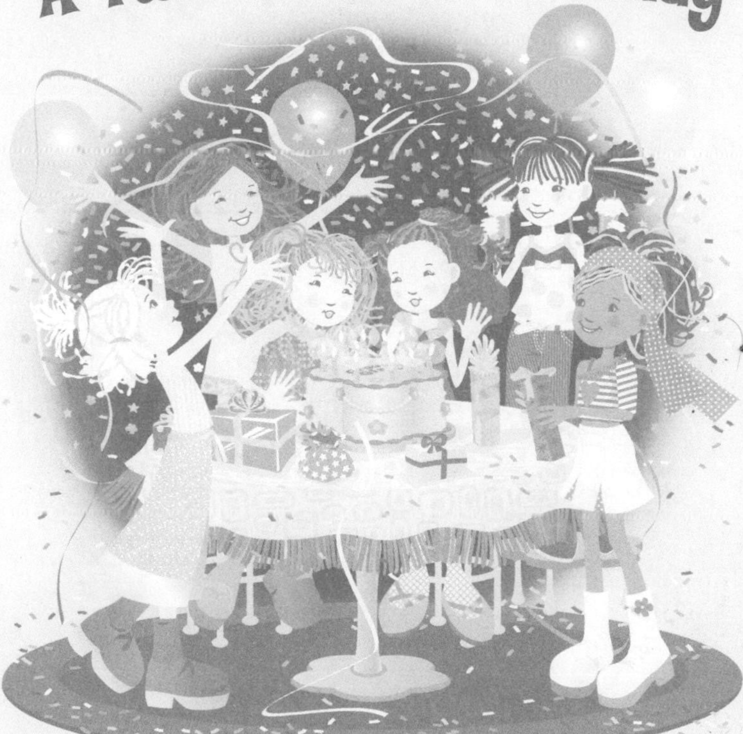

Robin Epstein

Scholastic Inc.

New York Toronto London Auckland Sydney
Mexico City New Delhi Hong Kong Buenos Aires

Read all the books about the Groovy Girls!

To my big sister, Amy, the girl who taught me
to scoop poop with a smile!

Cover illustration by Taia Morley
Interior illustrations by Bill Alger, Doug Day,
Kurt Marquart, and Yancey Labat

ISBN 0-439-81433-2

12 11 10 9 8 7 6 5 4 3 2   5 6 7 8 9 10/0

Printed in the U.S.A.
First Little Apple printing, September 2005

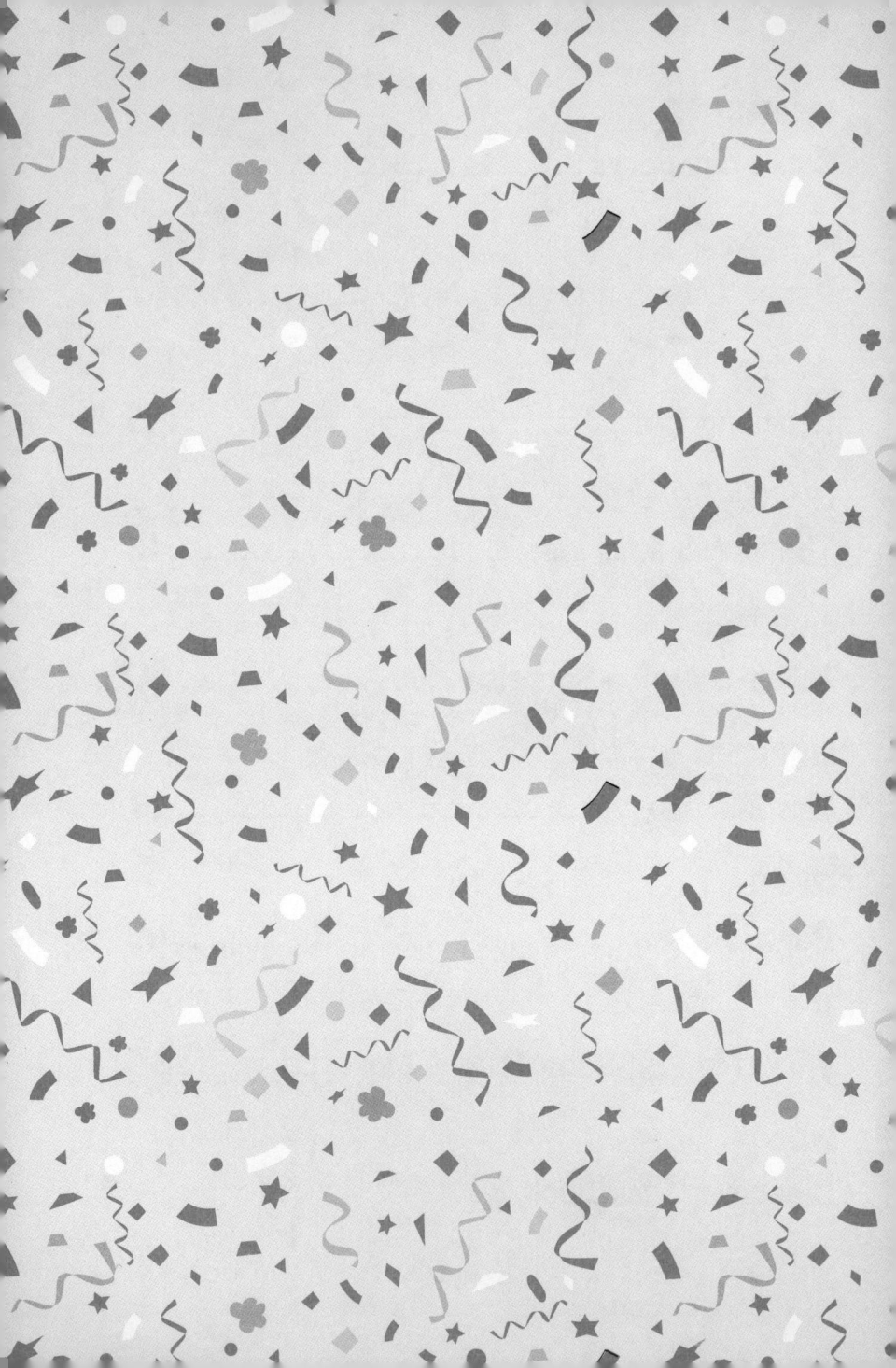

Chapter 1

Super Snoopers

"Shhhush!" Reese said loudly to her twin sister, O'Ryan, as the girls snooped through their mother's bedroom closet. "Do you *want* us to get caught?"

"Hey, it's not exactly like I was *trying* to make her shoe hit me on the head…then hit a box… then crash to the floor," O'Ryan replied.

"I don't get it! It's only three days till our birthday," Reese added, as she sifted through

Mom's sneakers, stacked heels, and ballerina flats. "So why can't we find our B-day presents?"

"I know. There should be LOTS of presents for us to find by now," O'Ryan responded.

Reese agreed. "Double digits should *definitely* mean double presents."

There was no doubt the girls were going to find their birthday treasures eventually.

After all, the twins were expert snoopers.

They could find a needle in a haystack (as long as that needle had "To O'Ryan and Reese" engraved on it).

In fact, each year the girls made a list of the gifts they thought they might be getting. And with that list, they could better imagine where their parents could hide something based on its size!

The list was made of three columns:

DEFINITE GETS	LIKELY POSSIBILITIES	NO WAY, IT'LL NEVER HAPPEN, BUT A GIRL CAN DREAM, CAN'T SHE?
🌸 Vintage t-shirts	🌸 Peacock feather earrings	🌸 Plane tickets to Alaska

"Wait a second!" Reese yelled. "I think I see something!" She reached her arm deep into the back of the closet. "What's this?"

Reese pulled out a small box with strawberry-print wrapping paper on it and a big silky bow.

"Shake it," O'Ryan instructed.

"Okay, that provided exactly zero info," Reese said. "I think we should investigate a little further."

Luckily, she was one crafty unwrapper!

She turned the strawberry-papered box over and slowly slid her finger under the seam to lift the tape. Once she'd successfully removed the paper, Reese opened the box top and the girls saw…

A pair of bulky, brown woolen socks?

"*What?*" O'Ryan said in disbelief.

Not only weren't these socks snazzy, they were a "zero" on the scale of groov-i-tude.

And, they were *E-normous*!

They were socks for Bigfoot.

"Wait a second," Reese said. "There's a card in here."

"Read it!" O'Ryan demanded.

"It says, 'Dear O'Ryan and Reese, nice try! But this *isn't* a gift for you.

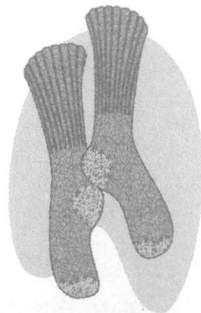

It's for Grandma Gertie. So, please rewrap this present and put it back where you found it. Love, Mom.'"

"Got to hand it to her," O'Ryan admitted. "Mom's getting good."

"Thank you," Mom replied, walking into her bedroom and catching the twins mid-snoop.

"Oh, Mom! We were just—" Reese stammered.

"Yes, I can see that," Mom said, smiling. "I'm sorry to disappoint you, girls, but your gift isn't in here. In fact, it's not even in the house yet."

"Do you think she means it?" O'Ryan whispered to Reese as Mom left the room.

"No way," Reese replied, shaking her head. "She probably just said that to throw us off the trail."

"And if Mom and Dad are being so smart about this, we need to be, too," O'Ryan said. "We've gotta go back to our size-finder list."

But as she started walking out of their parents' room, Reese stopped her sister.

"Hey," Reese said, "we can't leave their room looking like this."

O'Ryan glanced around and saw that she and Reese had made quite a mess of things.

"Okay," O'Ryan said. "Let's get everything

cleaned up in here. Then let's hit the list."

The girls put everything back in place perfectly. They even did a little extra organizing to make up for getting caught.

When they were done, the twins ran back to their own room.

"Okay, first thing tomorrow we start searching the coat closet downstairs for boxes of clothes," Reese said.

"Right, and where would they hide a hair straightener?"

"Or a video game?"

"Or a puppy?"

"Or Rollerblades?"

The girls kept adding gift possibilities to their list, trying to figure out the perfect hiding place for each one. And even though they didn't really expect it, they didn't rule out the possibility that there'd be a cute little pink Corvette waiting for them in the garage when they looked there first thing tomorrow morning!

Vrooooommmmm!

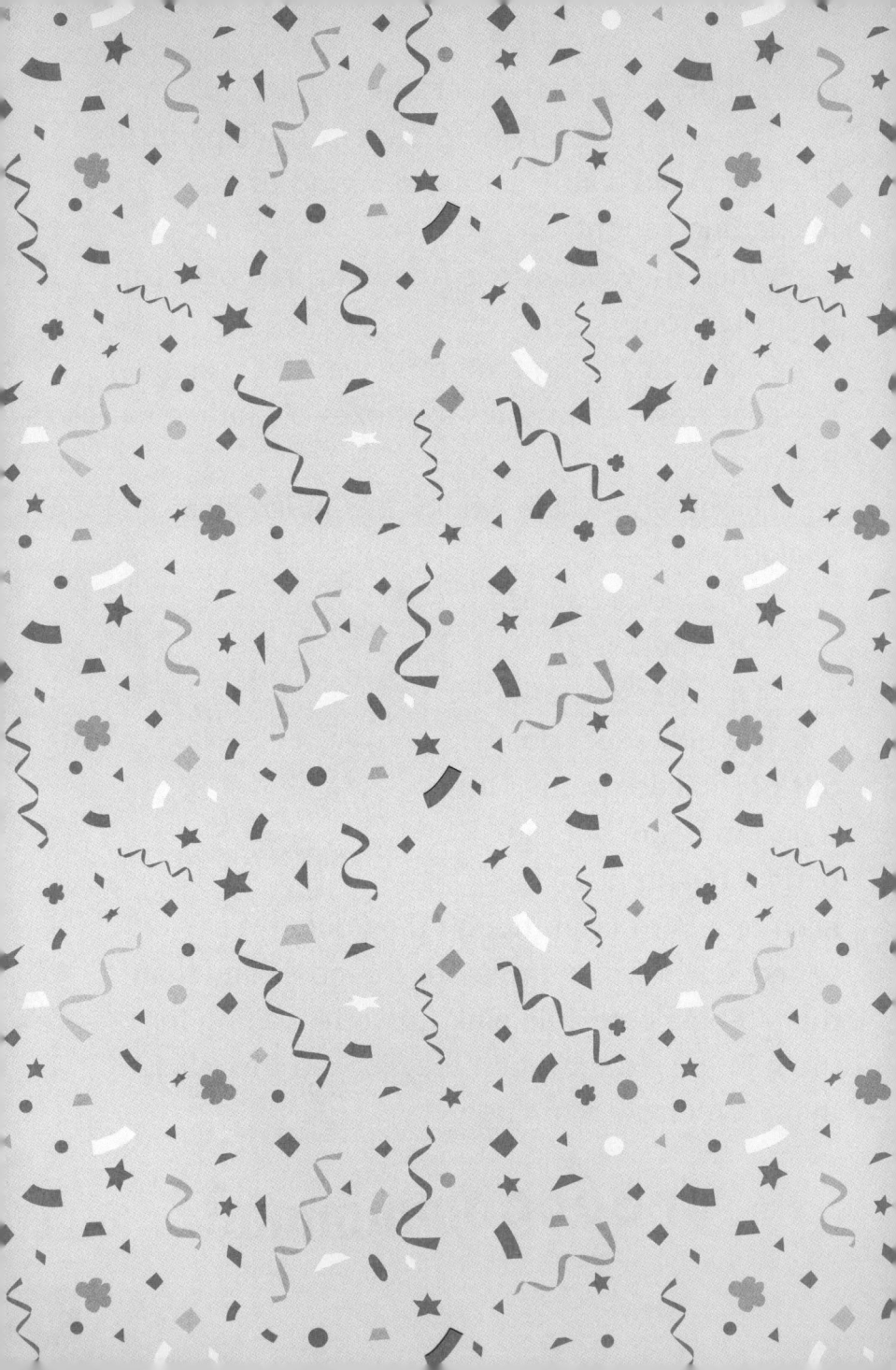

Chapter 2

Puppy Love

"Okay—who laid an egg?" O'Ryan asked as she and Reese walked into class the next morning.

"O'Ryan, don't be gross!" Reese giggled. "Maybe Mrs. Pearlman just wants us to have an *eggs-cellent* day."

Mysteriously, an egg sat in the pencil slot of each student's desk, with each of their initials on it.

And next to each egg, a tag read: HANDLE ME WITH CARE!

"Yay, breakfast!" Gwen yelled, seeing the eggs when she came running into the classroom a moment later. "I was running late—as usual—so I didn't get a chance to eat yet," she explained.

"Well, then eat up, Gwen," Oki replied. "'Cause you know what they say, 'an egg a day keeps the chickens away!'"

"Who says *that*?" O'Ryan asked.

But before Oki could give her *eggs*-planation, Mrs. P. entered the classroom.

"Good morning, class!" she said, carefully closing the door behind her. "Please take your seats...but do so ver-ry gent-ly!" she added, pointing to the eggs.

"Are we doing an egg toss?" O'Ryan asked. "That game is so fun!"

"No, O'Ryan," Mrs. Pearlman replied. "These eggs aren't for a game. They're for our next social studies unit. It's called 'Being a Responsible Citizen.'"

Oki rolled her eyes at O'Ryan, and O'Ryan's eyes rolled right back.

NOT fun, both girls thought.

"You see," Mrs. Pearlman continued, "being responsible is a big, important idea, and it means everything from doing homework, to taking out the garbage, to voting (when you're an adult), to taking care of our planet, and to caring for one another."

"So what does that have to do with eggs?" Reese asked.

"Well, when you take care of an egg, it can take care of you."

"You mean like giving us food?" Gwen said.

"Or more chickens?" Oki called out.

"Which means more food!" Gwen replied.

"That's right," Mrs. Pearlman said. "But to get the benefits from an egg, you need to handle it with care, right? Almost like it's a newborn baby. So for the next week, each of you will be responsible for taking care of the egg on your desk."

"So it's like our...egg baby?" O'Ryan asked.

"An egg baby?" Gwen repeated with delight. "Are you yolking?"

"Nope, no yolk!" Mrs. P. laughed. "Your assignment is to tend to that egg, making sure it doesn't crack or break. You'll have to watch it all the time, and take it with you everywhere you go."

"Wait. We're supposed to take our egg babies *everywhere*?" Reese asked.

"If you think about it, your parents are responsible for you twenty-four hours a day!

Being responsible is a full-time job," Mrs. P. said.

"But what if we have to do something where we can't be with them, Mrs. P.?" Oki called out.

"Well, class, what do parents do when they can't watch their children?"

"They turn on the TV set," O'Ryan replied. "Or, they get a babysitter, right?"

"Exactly. You find someone you trust to look after your child," Mrs. P. answered. "Because being a responsible citizen means making sure things are being taken care of."

"Sounds like a lot of work," Reese said.

"At first it may seem that way, Reese," Mrs. Pearlman said. "But hopefully, it will become second nature to you quickly. It's like getting to school on time. Or bringing in the mail. Or taking care of your little brother, or a pet."

Mrs. Pearlman opened the door to the classroom. "To teach us a little more about responsibility, I've invited a special guest to class today. She's right outside...Maggie?"

But Maggie didn't enter.

"Guess she's a little shy," Oki said to O'Ryan.

"Maggie, come on, girl!" Mrs. Pearlman repeated, this time slapping her hands against her thighs.

Everyone in the class looked around.

This seemed a weird way to talk to a guest!

Who is this mysterious Maggie girl?

And then came a jingling sound.

And a moment later, the mystery was solved!

Because Maggie, a bouncy, tan-colored cocker spaniel, came bounding into the classroom.

"Maggie's a doggy?" Reese asked excitedly.

And sure enough, tail wagging, body wiggling, and tongue hanging out, Maggie pranced up to the front of the classroom after Mrs. Pearlman.

"Is that your pooch, Mrs. P.?" O'Ryan asked.

"Yes, she is," Mrs. Pearlman replied, stroking the dog's ears.

"Look at how silky her coat is!" Oki said.

"She's so friendly," O'Ryan added.

"And happy!" Reese chimed in.

"And frisky!" Oki noted.

Gwen had gotten out of her chair, along with everyone else, when Maggie came into the class. But instead of going to the front of the room, she headed straight to the back.

"Is everything okay, Gwen?" Mrs. Pearlman

asked when she looked up.

"Uh, yeah, sorta," Gwen replied. "But, um, is that dog going to be here all day?"

"No," Mrs. Pearlman answered. "I'm taking her back home at lunch."

"Good," Gwen said under her breath. "Can I go to the nurse now? I'm not feeling so well."

"Of course you can," Mrs. Pearlman replied. "Here, take the hall pass." Mrs. P. walked over to her desk to get the fluorescent orange paddle. But when she started walking to the back of the classroom to hand it to Gwen, Maggie began to follow her.

"Maybe you can just throw it to me," Gwen said quickly.

Mrs. Pearlman nodded. "Reese, since you're closer to Gwen than I am, can you pass this to her?"

"Sure," Reese replied, taking the hall pass from Mrs. P. and walking it back to Gwen. "I hope you feel better," Reese said. "I didn't even *know* you were sick."

"It happened kind of suddenly," Gwen said. "I'm sure I'll feel better by lunch."

"Wait!" Reese cried out. "Don't forget your egg baby!"

"Oh, yeah," Gwen replied. She walked back over to her desk, and just as she was picking up her egg, Maggie barked. "WHOA!" Gwen said, fumbling with the egg. As soon as she got control of it again, she ran out of the classroom.

"So how come your dog's visiting on egg–baby day?" Oki asked.

"Because," Mrs. Pearlman replied, "my Maggie is about to have some babies of her own. And soon she'll have a whole litter of puppies to take care of. Which is what you call a whole lot of responsibility!"

"But Maggie and I can't take care of all of those pups ourselves. We're going to need some help."

"We can help!" Reese said. "We'll take a puppy home."

"That may be possible, but you'll need to talk about that with your parents first," replied Mrs. P.

"If we can get permission, we can get a pup?" asked O'Ryan.

"Well, not so fast. Your egg babies are also going to help me decide who'd be responsible enough to have a dog," said Mrs. Pearlman.

Huh?

"You see, at the end of this project," Mrs. P. explained, "you're all going to tell us about your experiences with your egg."

"Cool!" Oki said.

"In an essay," Mrs. Pearlman added.

"Less cool," Oki replied.

Reese looked at O'Ryan, and O'Ryan looked at Reese.

And they both knew *eggs-actly* what the other one was thinking.

It was: *I WANT A DOG!!!*

And suddenly both twins knew what they wanted for their birthday more than anything else.

More than a drum set.

More than a hair straightener.

More than a video game.

(Well, truth be told, they were still hoping to get all those things, too.)

But what they really, *really* wanted—more than *any*thing else—was something that didn't even come wrapped with a bow. What they wanted was: Parental Permission for a Pearlman Puppy!

Chapter 3
Cracking Up!

"Your egg baby's wearing a hair bow!" Reese exclaimed when she saw Gwen and her egg sitting at the table in the cafeteria. "How cute!"

"I made it with some gauze I got in the nurse's office," Gwen said, as Reese, O'Ryan, and Oki took their seats next to her.

"Very groovy, Gwen!" Oki nodded with approval, cradling her own egg in her hands.

"And practical!" Gwen grinned. "'Cause the gauze bow also doubles as a helmet, just in case Eggsmerelda—that's what I named her—falls!"

As the girls laughed, Vanessa and Yvette walked over to the table carrying their trays.

"Hey, careful!" O'Ryan exclaimed as the older girls put their trays down. "We don't want to make an omelet here!"

"Oh!" Vanessa said. "So you guys are doing the unit on Responsibility, huh?"

"We did that last year," Yvette added, taking her seat. "It was a good one."

"Are you feeling better?" Reese asked her best friend, Gwen, interrupting the other conversation.

"Much better!" Gwen answered. "Thanks."

Then she added: "I wasn't really feeling sick when I asked to go to the nurse."

"I *knew* you were faking!" O'Ryan said. "You went from zero to sickly pretty fast!"

"Hey, I wasn't *totally* faking," Gwen replied. "I mean I *did* have a stomach ache. I'm just not sure I want to tell you why."

"You can tell us," Reese said, leaning in.

"Well," Gwen hesitated. "Well…the truth is… my stomach hurt 'cause of Maggie."

"Maggie?" Vanessa repeated.

"Mrs. P. brought her dog to class," Reese explained to Vanessa and Yvette.

"You mean you were scared of Mrs. Pearlman's cocker spaniel?" Oki asked.

Gwen nodded. "Dogs freak me out."

"No kidding?" Reese asked. "I never knew that."

"Well, it's not *exactly* something I brag about," Gwen replied.

"That's so weird, 'cause I love dogs," Reese said. She just assumed if she adored dogs, her best friend would, too.

"We're going to try to convince our parents to let us have one of Mrs. Pearlman's puppies for our birthday!" O'Ryan said. "*Which*, by the way, is in exactly two—count 'em, *one, two*—days! Just so none of you forgets!"

"Oh, I'm sure you'll get a puppy for your birthday," Gwen replied.

"Why would you say something like that, Gwen?" Vanessa asked sharply.

"I mean you have to be pretty mature to take care of a dog," Yvette added quickly.

"We know." Reese frowned. "We've wanted one for practically forever. But our parents *always* say we aren't ready."

"But," O'Ryan said, turning to her twin, "how

can they possibly say that about us this year? At ten, we're going to be *way* old enough!"

"Yeah, but it's not like you guys are going to be turning eleven—like Yvette and me," Vanessa replied smugly.

Yvette nodded and smiled at Vanessa. "Yep. Turning eleven *is* a whole 'nother level."

"'Cause when you turn eleven that means you're practically thir*teen*."

"But!" Gwen smiled. "Even though you guys are only turning ten—like I'm going to be at my next birthday, and Oki, too—I'm *sure* your parents think you're mature enough to handle a dog now!"

"Really?" Reese asked. "You really think so?"

"Definitely," Gwen said, and was just about to add that she was a-thousand-million-times totally sure, but stopped herself when she saw Vanessa raise her eyebrows at her, and Yvette shake her head.

"It's not good to get their hopes up, Gwen," Vanessa scolded.

"And making them think their parents will let them get a dog is *not* a very mature thing to do," Yvette added.

"Hey, lay off! Gwen was just trying to make the twins feel better," Oki said, jumping up from her chair to make the point.

But when Oki pulled out her chair, she forgot something...she forgot about her egg baby.

And in just that instant, it started to roll...

"Nooooooo!" Oki yelled, frozen to the spot as she pictured her egg baby turning into Humpty Dumpty!

But just before the egg crashed to the floor, Gwen dove for it.

"Got him!" Gwen cried out.

"Oh, thanks!" Oki said, taking her egg baby back from Gwen and stroking its shell. "That was a close call."

"I guess you'll know to be more careful next time," Vanessa said to Oki.

"Yeah," Yvette nodded. "You'll learn."

Oki looked at the two older girls and narrowed

her eyes. "Just because you guys are in fifth grade doesn't mean you know everything!"

"Well, obviously we're mature enough to know how to take care of an egg baby better than you," Vanessa responded.

Uh-oh.

"Hey! Hey! Girls!" Gwen said quickly, hoping to break the tension. "We're upsetting the eggs. And Oki,"  Gwen said, using a pretend grown–up voice, "the older girls didn't mean any harm. 'Cause seriously, how could anyone think we're immature?" And as she said this, Gwen put an enormous orange rind between her lips.

Then she gave a big orangutan smile.

Reese started laughing first.

Then O'Ryan.

A moment later, Oki couldn't help it: She was giggling, too.

Then both Vanessa and Yvette joined in—how could they not?

And before they knew it, all the Groovy Girls were laughing together like happy little monkeys!

Chapter 4

The Worst Best Idea

"**I** have the best idea!" Reese said as the twins walked home from soccer practice that afternoon.

"If you're gonna say that we should do extra homework today so we won't have any on our birthday weekend, don't!" O'Ryan replied.

"Nooo!" Reese said, rolling her eyes. "I'm talking about doing something to earn us a puppy!"

"Oh, okay, I'm listening," O'Ryan replied.

"I think we should show Mom and Dad that we're 'responsible citizens.' 'Cause if we can do that, I bet they'd give us permission to get a dog."

"Wow," O'Ryan responded, "that actually *is* a good idea! What should we do?"

"Well, we could repaint Mom and Dad's bedroom," Reese suggested.

"With what?" O'Ryan asked.

"We've got a lot of glitter nail polish—it could be really pretty," Reese said.

"Oh! *Or*," O'Ryan said excitedly, "maybe we could get Dad a new car from eBay?!"

"That would be superrific!"

By now the twins had reached home, and they stopped to bang out their cleats, which were caked in mud, before going in. Mom hated getting mud tracks on the floor, so the girls wanted to be sure to clean their shoes off really, really well today. But first, they put their backpacks down *ver-ry care-fully* because their eggs were in them.

"Hey, do you think there's something we can do tonight—like at dinner—to show them we're responsible?" O'Ryan asked Reese.

"Tonight's spaghetti night, isn't it? So, why don't we make dinner?"

"Yeah! We could totally do that," O'Ryan exclaimed. "We've watched Mom make spaghetti every Thursday for practically our whole lives!"

But when the girls got to the kitchen, Mom was already mid-spaghetti prep.

"We're here to help!" Reese said.

"Really? How fabulous!" Mom replied. Then she added, "But I can tell you, your birthday presents aren't hidden in the kitchen cabinets."

"We know that already!" Reese responded.

"Yeah, we looked in them yesterday," O'Ryan said, so only her twin could hear. But then she added, "See, Reese and I want to help because, you know, the two of us are getting older. And we're, like, *very* responsible now."

"Okay." Mom smiled. "Good to know."

"I'm gonna set the table and make it really nice," Reese exclaimed, climbing up on the counter.

But when Mom saw Reese grabbing Grandma's fine china, she gasped. "You know what?" Mom said quickly. "Let's just use our regular plates tonight."

"Oh, okay," Reese said, jumping back down.

"I'll stir the sauce!" O'Ryan cried out, taking the wooden spoon from the drawer. "And now, some music to cook by!" She banged the spoon on the counter until she reached the pot. Then she began stirring with great gusto.

Problem was, O'Ryan's gusto was *much more robust-o* than the sauce in the pot.

And by stirring so *strongly*, she caused a tidal wave of tomato matter.

Sauce splattered EV-ER-Y-WHERE.

It got on the countertop.

It got on O'Ryan's shirt.

And some even splashed on O'Ryan's bangs!

"Good thing you've got red hair," Mom said, trying not to laugh when she saw the mess.

"Yeah," O'Ryan said. Normally something like this would have made her laugh, too. But she didn't think giggling would make her sound very *responsible*—which would only make their puppy-getting-permission-slip mission even harder.

"O'Ryan, you're planning to clean that up, aren't you?" Reese quickly asked. But Reese wasn't *really* asking. It was more like she was *telling* her sister to clean up the mess.

"You bet I'm going to clean it up," O'Ryan replied. "I'm very responsible like that," she added glancing over at her mother.

"Know what, Mom?" Reese said. "I think we have this under control. So why don't you go rest now? O'Ryan and I will call you and Dad to dinner when everything's ready."

"And we'll make a salad, too!" O'Ryan added.

"Okay," Mom replied. "I'll just drain the spaghetti and put it in a bowl. And you guys can bring it to the table when everything else is ready."

"Thanks, Mom!" both girls said together.

"You're welcome," Mom said, amused by the two helpful workers who had replaced her daughters. "And thank *you*!"

After O'Ryan and Reese finished setting the kitchen table together—and threw lettuce on some plates for salad— they were ready.

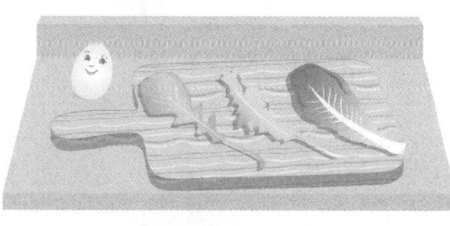

"COME 'N GET IT!" O'Ryan shouted.

"O'Ryan!" Reese scolded. "Don't do it like that. You need to make it sound *adult-i-er*."

But their folks must have been ready because they came running in to the kitchen anyway!

"I hear I'm in for quite a treat," Dad said, smiling at the twins.

"You just sit down, Dad, and we'll serve you!" O'Ryan replied.

"Yeah," Reese said. "Just leave it to your supreme servers. We can take care of everything!"

Both girls were *so* excited, they started fighting over who got to carry the spaghetti bowl to the table. (They forgot about the sauce.)

"I should take it," O'Ryan said. "I'm older."

"Only by seven minutes," Reese replied.

"And, anyway, it was my idea to help!" Reese added, pushing her sister away.

"Reese, let go!" O'Ryan said.

"No, you!" Reese shouted back, pulling the bowl toward her.

"You!" said O'Ryan, grabbing it back.

"You!" replied Reese, holding on to its side.

As each girl pushed and pulled, the spaghetti decided it would get to the table all by itself.

The bowl went *flying*!

And with it, each and every strand of spaghetti hit the floor.

"Smooth move, O'Ryan," Reese whispered.

"Real responsible, Reese," O'Ryan whispered right back.

"Uh, but don't worry, Mom and Dad!" Reese added quickly. "We'll get this mess cleaned up in a jiff."

"Yeah, 'cause that's how responsible we are!" O'Ryan said, smiling with all her teeth.

"Why don't I just throw some burgers on the grill in the meantime," Dad said, since the spaghetti dinner was all but over. He was trying hard not to laugh. Mom too. They both actually thought the whole thing was pretty funny, but they didn't want the girls to be upset.

"I can pat the meat into burger shapes," O'Ryan said.

"Know what, girls?" Mom replied with a smile. "I think you've *both* helped enough for one night!"

Reese looked at O'Ryan, and O'Ryan looked at Reese. And both girls knew exactly what the other was thinking: *WE BLEW IT! We were completely irresponsible!*

The burgers grilled quickly, so no one starved for *too* long. But even though the girls both loved Dad's hamburgers, that night neither one could finish her meal.

"We messed up big-time," Reese said to O'Ryan as she put the leftovers back into the fridge after dinner. "We were crazy kitchen klutzes."

"Yeah," O'Ryan replied, "we'll never get that puppy for our birthday now."

"Wow, and look at this!" Mom said, coming back into the kitchen. "You girls are even cleaning up? Without being asked?!"

The girls nodded.

"Well, this is a nice surprise! And speaking of surprises, I was going to keep *this* under wraps, but on Saturday—which, I believe, just also happens to be your birthday—we'll be going on a road trip with your friends."

"Really?" Reese said, instantly brightening.

"Where are we going?" O'Ryan asked excitedly.

"Well, I can't tell you *that*!" Mom replied, smiling. "That would ruin the surprise, wouldn't it?" Then she added, "You'll just have to wait till Saturday to find out."

"A surprise road trip?" O'Ryan repeated to Reese when the girls were alone.

"What do you think we're gonna do?" Reese asked.

"I don't know. But I think I know how we can figure it out!" O'Ryan said. "Back to the list!"

The twins took their egg babies, which had been sitting quietly on the counter, and ran upstairs. After they rested the eggs on their desks, Reese grabbed a notepad and a pencil. On the notepad she made three lists.

"I think London!" said O'Ryan.

"I think France!" said Reese.

Likely places to go on a road trip

Places it would be groovy to go on a road trip

Places I've always dreamed of going on a road trip, but might take a plane to get to

O'Ryan really was trying to act mature, but enough was enough, and she decided she needed a break from maturity. So she couldn't help adding, "I think I see your underpants!"

Chapter 5
A Loo-Loo of a Surprise

"**S**o, do you know how long it's gonna take to get to Rinky Dink Junction?" Gwen asked Reese as the two friends played at the McCloud's the next day after school—just one day before the twins' birthday.

Reese had just told Gwen that she'd heard about the birthday road trip.

"Rinky Dink Junction?" Reese repeated. "So *that's* where we're going, huh?"

Gwen instantly realized her mistake. And she worried she'd just blown the surprise.

"Rinky Dink Junction?" Gwen replied, panicking. "Uh, no. We're not going there. Why would you think that?" Gwen hoped if she denied it, maybe Reese would forget what she had said.

"I'm asking because you JUST SAID that's where we're going!" Reese smiled. "Oh, I can't wait to tell Mom and Dad I found out where we're going."

"Please, no!" Gwen cried. "You can't. You can't tell anyone I told you about going to Rinky Dink."

"Why not?"

"'Cause nobody thinks I can keep a secret. And if you tell them I told you, that'll just prove them right." Gwen shook her head.

When Reese realized Gwen wasn't kidding, she said, "All right, I promise not to tell anyone— except O'Ryan, okay?"

"Thanks, babe!" Gwen said, hugging her friend.

Reese hugged Gwen right back, then ran upstairs to find her sister. And as soon as Reese spilled Gwen's info, O'Ryan went directly to the computer.

"So, let's find out what we're going to see in Rinky Dink," O'Ryan exclaimed, clapping her hands.

Gwen bit her nails as O'Ryan typed, nervous about what the girls might find on the screen. But Gwen saw that there was some good news (at least at first) because O'Ryan turned out to be as bad a speller as she was!

"R-I-N-K-E-E D-O-N-K," O'Ryan pecked on the keyboard.

No Results for Rinkee Donk, the monitor read.

"It's not Rinkee Donk, it's Rinky Dink, you ding-a-ling," Reese said, pushing O'Ryan right off the keyboard. "World Wide Web, don't fail me now," Reese added after she'd correctly typed in the name of the town.

The first link that came up was for an Irish rock band.

"That can't be it," O'Ryan said.

Next one was for an apron-making company in Ohio. "Nope, that's not it, either," Reese added.

Then...pay dirt!

Link number three was an entry for Large Lou's Museum of Loo-Loos, located at Rinky Dink Junction in the town of Rinky Dink!

"What in the world is Large Lou's Museum of Loo-Loos?" Reese asked as she clicked on the link.

"Welcome to Large Lou's Museum of Loo-Loos!" a voice boomed through the computer speakers. "Located in the heart of Rinky Dink, right at the junction, our museum features the World's Largest Stuff EVER!"

The pictures on the site showed a twenty-foot-tall papier-mâché gorilla standing next to a ten-foot-tall banana.

There was a gigantic roller skate, too.

And a HUGE can of spray cheese.

Then the computer voice started speaking again.

"And remember, moms and dads, Large Lou's Museum of Loo-Loos is a great place to host a birthday party for your kids! Little ones love it!"

"Holy cow!" Reese said.

"They're throwing us a kiddie party at Large Lou's?!" O'Ryan asked Gwen in disbelief.

"Uh," Gwen said, biting her lip. "You can't make me say any more! Believe whatever you want. But just remember, I didn't tell you an-y-thing!"

"We know," Reese replied, sounding supremely

disappointed. "I just can't believe that *this* is what Mom and Dad think of us. They still think we're little kids who want a little-kiddie party!"

"Aw, come on," Gwen giggled. "You have to admit that can of spray cheese *is* kind of fun."

"But that's not the point!" Reese said.

"The *point*," O'Ryan continued, finishing her twin's thought, "is that if Mom and Dad think this is what we'd like, they don't think we're very mature."

"And if they don't think we're mature," Reese continued, "they don't think we're responsible."

"And if they don't think we're responsible," O'Ryan added, "they won't agree to let us get one of Mrs. Pearlman's puppies."

"Oh," Gwen nodded. "I get your drift now."

"We've got to make them change their minds about this somehow," O'Ryan said.

"Maybe we could just drop hints about how much we hope we're not going to a dumb museum," Reese replied. "So they'll know we wouldn't want to go to one."

"No, that won't work. That'll just make us seem even younger," O'Ryan said. "'Cause old people actually like ALL kinds of museums."

"She's right," Gwen replied. "Old people are mad for museums."

Okay. Think. Think. Think.

"Wait!" O'Ryan exclaimed. "What if we use this to our advantage?"

"What are you talking about?" Reese asked.

"What if we go along with the idea? Make believe we think going to a stupid museum is the greatest thing in the world."

"Why would we do that?"

"Because, little sister, mature people pretend to like things they don't like *all the time*!"

"But that's kind of like lying, isn't it?" Reese replied.

"Totally. Which is very mature!" O'Ryan assured her twin. "I mean, you know how Dad always says he loves Grandma's meatloaf, and we really know he hates it?"

"Oh, yeah!" Reese nodded, suddenly understanding. "And like Mom told Uncle Ben she thought his new tie was really nice, when we knew she thought it was tacky!"

"And she was right about that!" O'Ryan laughed.

"So what are you guys going to do?" Gwen asked.

"We're going to start playing along," Reese said.

"We're going to pretend to be really surprised and really happy that we're going to this silly museum for our birthday," O'Ryan nodded.

"Man," Reese exclaimed, "I'm feeling older and wiser already!"

O'Ryan walked to the mirror over her bureau. "A gigantic gorilla, how splendid!" she said, practicing her "surprise" face.

"Why, yes. How absolutely deee-lightful!" Reese added, joining O'Ryan at the mirror. "A giant can of spray cheese is what I call fine art!"

As maturely as possible, the twins smiled at each other's reflection.

Who knew "acting" mature could be so easy and so much fun!

Chapter 6

The BIG Day

HA-PPY B-DAY!" Oki said excitedly to O'Ryan and Reese Saturday morning.

After 364 days of waiting, it was Reese and O'Ryan's birthday at last.

HA-PPY B-DAY!" Gwen yelled as she ran up the walkway a little later. "I woulda been here sooner, but I forgot Eggsmerelda, and I had to go back home and get her."

Gwen put her egg baby down and hugged Reese. Oki did the same—but hugged O'Ryan.

Then the huggers switched.

"So how does it feel to be double digits?" Oki asked.

"Superrific!" O'Ryan replied.

"Fanta*bulous*," Reese said, as their parents joined them. "As a matter of fact, as soon as O'Ryan woke up today I could see that she looked *even more* mature than she did yesterday!"

"Yeah," O'Ryan nodded, "and Reese looked much more responsible to me. But that's what being ten's all about!"

"Okay, you guys ready to go?" Reese asked.

"Well, we have to wait for Vanessa and Yvette, don't we?" Oki said.

"Actually, they're not going to be coming with us," O'Ryan replied.

"Why not?" Oki asked, crossing her arms.

"Well, when Vanessa called to wish us a happy birthday," O'Ryan said, "she told us that she and Yvette had some other stuff to do today."

"Oh," Oki said, shaking her head.

She couldn't believe it! Vanessa and Yvette had flaked. And Oki just bet it had something to do with that lunch on Thursday—when the fifth grade friends said how much more *mature* they were than the fourth graders.

"Well, you know what?" Gwen replied. "It's just too bad that those girls are going to be missing out on our fun. I mean, look!" Gwen said, holding up a picnic basket that she'd brought.

"Food for the road!" Oki explained. "Sticky-sweet breakfast stuff!"

"Oh, that's so supreme of you guys," Reese said.

"Well, let's get going," O'Ryan said.

As soon as they hopped in the car and were on their way, the girls broke out their sweet treats.

"Gwen, your cinnamon buns are scrump-dilly-umptious!" Reese said, licking her lips.

"Tank you veddy much!" Gwen replied crunching down on a handful of cereal. "And I love the way Oki put five different kinds of cereal in these lunch bags she decorated for us."

The girls crunched and munched and munched and crunched till they'd stuffed themselves silly.

After much chatting, many games of I Spy, and what seemed like *hundreds* of rounds of singing "Ninety-Nine Bottles of Pop on the Wall," a big billboard came into view on the side of the road.

"Welcome to Rinky Dink," O'Ryan read. "Home of Large Lou's Museum of Loo-Loos."

"Gee," Reese said, trying her best to seem surprised, "that sounds interesting! Doesn't it, O'Ryan?"

"Sure does," O'Ryan replied. "What's that?" she added, pointing to the giant gorilla and hamming it up.

"Looks like great art!" Reese replied.

Gwen couldn't help herself—she started giggling. And she laughed even harder at the surprised looks on the twins' faces when the car sped right past Large Lou's Museum of Loo-Loos!

"Huh?" O'Ryan replied. "What's going on?"

And both girls were even more confused when the car finally stopped in the driveway of an old farmhouse.

"Look at all the hay!" Gwen shouted.

Then, suddenly, it dawned on Reese why their parents had brought them to a place like this...and it was worse than she ever could have imagined! Worse even than the kiddie party they had mistakenly expected at Large Lou's Museum of Loo-Loos.

"Hay rides?!" she said, with undisguised disappointment. "We're going on hay rides?!"

Even though Reese and O'Ryan wanted to play it cool, the idea that their parents thought they'd like something like this—something even more babyish than a party at Loo-Loos—was just too much!

"Aren't we a bit old for hay rides?" O'Ryan asked.

"Hey, what's wrong with hay rides?" Gwen said.

"Yeah, I think they're fun, too," Oki added.

"Well, it's just that we didn't think we'd be doing them on our birthday," Reese said, trying to regain her fast-fading sense of maturity.

"Hay rides?" Mom said, turning around to face the girls. "Who said anything about hay rides?"

"Yeah," Dad replied, "maybe you girls should just hop out of the car and see what the rest of this farm has to offer."

"Okay," O'Ryan said, unbuckling her seat belt and opening the door.

"I'm just gonna stay in the car," Gwen said. "So you can leave your egg babies here with me."

Reese looked at Gwen, but before she had time to say anything, she heard a loud barking sound. Then a very friendly copper-colored dog trotted out from behind the barn to greet her. It was a gorgeous golden retriever!

"Well, hello, doggy!" Reese said, petting the dog's lustrous long fur.

Oki and O'Ryan quickly joined Reese. And that's when the girls got their next surprise.

Ruff-ruff-ruff-ruff-ruff-ruff-ruff.

Pound-pound-pound-pound-pound.

Bark-bark-bark-bark-bark.

The sound of forty little puppy feet came rumbling toward them. And all those feet, attached to ten different puppies, crashed to a halt right next to the big mommy dog.

"Look at all these doggies!" O'Ryan said, as the girls thrilled at the sight of the playful pups.

"Yes, there usually are a lot of dogs at a puppy farm," Mom replied, smiling.

Reese and O'Ryan looked at each other. A puppy farm? The girls had heard of a horse farm. And a cow farm. And a chicken farm. But they'd never heard of a puppy farm...

And why would their parents have brought them to a puppy farm on their birthday?

"Girls," Dad said, "Mom and I have been amazed by how responsible you've become."

"You mean 'cause of the dinner we tried to make the other night?" Reese asked.

"Nope." Mom shook her head. "Not just because of that. But because of the little things you've been doing each and every day. Like helping to clear the table without being asked. Like taking care not to muddy up the rugs. Like even cleaning up our bedroom better than Dad and I had had it. For all those reasons, we think both of you have proven you're ready for a dog."

"Wait a minute!" Reese exclaimed. "So you're not joking? You're saying that we're really here to get a dog? Not just to *play* with them?"

"And you're saying that we've *earned* it?" O'Ryan added.

Mom and Dad nodded.

O'Ryan and Reese's mouths dropped open.

"REALLY?"

"Yes, really!" Dad said, a puppy nipping at his cuff.

The girls grabbed each other's hands and started jumping up and down. Which caused the puppies to get even more excited, turning them into a blur of yelping, panting, wagging fur!

"Wait!" Dad yelled. "Could you guys do that little dance again? My camcorder wasn't on yet!" But the girls didn't even have to be asked because they weren't going to stop dancing around any time soon!

"Ohmigosh! Look at how playful she is. We have to get this one!" O'Ryan said, petting one of the puppies.

But Reese had already picked up one of the other little ones. "No way, look at him. This guy's the most adorable thing I've ever seen." She tickled the puppy's belly, and the dog immediately started licking her face.

"No, mine's better!" O'Ryan insisted. She also couldn't help but notice that the puppy in her hands didn't seem to like Reese at all.

"Nuh-uh, mine!" Reese shouted right back. (Reese's dog had no interest in O'Ryan, either.)

"Maybe they can get *both*?" Oki asked, looking for a way to solve the problem.

"No, I'm sorry, girls, we can absolutely only take one," Mom answered.

"Well, then we should get mine. I'm older!" O'Ryan said.

"So what?" Reese replied.

"Guys," Oki said, "I think the maturity factor is dipping here."

Speaking of maturity, with all the excitement, everyone had forgotten about paying attention to Gwen.

Gwen, who was still sitting in the car with her seat belt on.

Mom knocked on one of the car windows, which was open just a tiny little bit. "Gwen, don't you want to come out and play with the puppies?"

Gwen shook her head. "No, thanks, I'm good. Besides, someone has to watch the egg babies."

Reese walked over to Mom and whispered, "Gwen's a little afraid of dogs."

"Oh." Mom nodded. "Well, maybe you could show her through the window how cuddly and friendly the puppies are. Puppies can sometimes seem a lot less scary than full-grown dogs."

"Yeah!" Reese said. "Hey, girls," she called to the others. "Let's show Gwen how nice-'n-not-scary these puppies are."

Oki and O'Ryan rushed over to the car, each carrying a squirmy little pup in her arms.

The dog in O'Ryan's arms looked like it was trying to lick Gwen's face clear through the window! And Gwen had to admit that holding that little doggy looked like it would be a lot of fun.

Reese's puppy wasn't moving around all that much—he just looked kind of tired. And sure enough, a minute later, he stretched out his paws and gave the cutest little puppy yawn you could imagine!

"He looks like me at the beginning of the school day!" Gwen exclaimed.

When Reese's puppy closed his brown eyes, Gwen rolled down her window some more.

"Do you think maybe I could pet him?" she asked.

"I think he'd like that a lot," Reese replied.

Gwen put her hand out, a little nervously at first, and stroked the dog's head as Reese held him.

"He's the softest thing I've ever touched!" Gwen said.

"I think he likes you," Reese replied. "Do you want to hold him?"

Gwen didn't say anything for a moment. She just stared at the sleepy little pup.

"Oki," Gwen finally said. "Do me a favor?"

"Sure," Oki replied.

"Could you watch the egg babies for a minute? I want to get out of the car to hold the puppy."

When Gwen took the puppy from Reese, O'Ryan suddenly realized that she could be very happy with that dog, too.

He was cuddly. He was friendly. He was quiet.

O'Ryan looked at Reese and smiled, and her seven-minutes-younger twin smiled right back.

After they'd talked to the breeder and officially bought that pup, along with a collar and leash, and a crate for him to sleep and travel in, the McClouds put the puppy in the back of the station wagon.

"So," Oki said to the twins, "what are you going to name him?"

"Henry," Reese said.

"Nuh-uh," O'Ryan replied, "he's totally a Max."

"No, he's not!"

"Yes, he is!"

And as the two *very mature* McCloud twins kept bickering all the way home, their now fully awake, frisky new puppy—whatever his name was—happily barked along with them!

Chapter 7

Party Pooper!

"**S**URRRRRPRRRRISSSSE!**" Reese and O'Ryan heard as they turned the knob to their front door.

"AAAHHHHH!" screamed the two VERY surprised twins.

"RUFFRUFFRUFF!" barked their over-excited new puppy.

"Happy surprise slumber party!" Yvette shouted, as she and Vanessa threw confetti at the girls.

While the others had been at the puppy farm, Vanessa and Yvette had stayed back to decorate the McClouds' house with paw-print balloons, puppy-wrapping-papered presents, and streamers.

The puppy ran around in little puppy circles, and then, without warning, *peed on the floor*!

"I think he needs to go outside," Reese said.

"I think it's a little late for that," O'Ryan responded. "Let's get something to clean up the puddle."

But when the girls walked into the kitchen, they got another not-so-little surprise!

Yvette's mom was holding a cake in the shape of a dog bone, brightly lit with ten candles and an extra candle for good luck!

"Happy birthday, girls!" Yvette's mom said as everyone broke out into a loud chorus of "Happy Birthday."

"Holy cow!" Reese exclaimed.

"Ohmigosh!" O'Ryan beamed.

As the twins approached the cake, their new puppy jumped around at their heels.

"Okay," O'Ryan said, "on the count of three."

"One," said Reese.

"Two," said O'Ryan.

"THREE!" the girls said. Then, closing their eyes to make their wishes, they blew out the candles.

Reese laughed when she opened her eyes. "I didn't even *know* what to wish for," she said.

"I mean, I already *got* exactly what I wanted!"

"I'd say that makes you a pretty lucky girl," Mom replied.

"Of course she's lucky," O'Ryan said. "She has *me* as an older sister."

"And *me* as a best friend," Gwen added.

"And *me* as a fashion consultant!" Oki smiled, flipping up Reese's collar.

"And *us* as super-duper party planners!" Vanessa chimed in.

"Which makes our puppy pretty lucky, too!" Reese said.

"Yeah, and I think he should be an honorary member of the Groovy Girls," O'Ryan nodded. "He'll be our group egg baby—only a real one!"

"With two mommies and four new aunties," Reese added.

The dog must have liked the idea, because he started running back and forth across the kitchen floor between them, slipping and sliding on the tiles.

"He's soooo precious," Vanessa said. "What are you going to call him?"

"Henry!" said Reese.

"Max!" said O'Ryan.

"I think you should call him Lacey," Yvette said.

"But Lacey's a girl's name. Why would they

want to call him that?" Gwen asked.

"'Cause look!" Yvette replied, pointing to the dog, who was now busy chewing the shoelaces on the pile of sneakers by the kitchen door.

"Puppy, no!" Reese yelled.

The puppy looked back at her with the saddest eyes and whimpered.

Reese felt terrible; she absolutely couldn't stay mad, so she changed her mind. "It's okay, you can chew the laces if you want," she said.

So much for parental discipline!

"Way to teach him a lesson, Reese!" O'Ryan said, shaking her head.

"Okay, *you* try punishing him then!"

O'Ryan looked at her new little puppy, who was happily chewing up her left sneaker. "That's okay," she said, laughing, "I need new kicks, anyway!"

"Come on, girls. Let's go back into the living room. The party's just starting!" Yvette said. "And what would our sleepovers be without PIZZA?!"

The girls made a beeline to the living room so they could have their cake—and eat pizza, too!

"Doggy, please!" Gwen said, trying to chew her slice while the puppy, who she had put in her lap, licked her face.

"Look at you, Gwen!" Reese said to her friend, proudly.

"I just think he's hungry," O'Ryan said, pulling a slice of pizza from the box and dangling it above the puppy. "Here ya go, Max. Jump!"

"Jump, Henry!" Reese said.

And boy, oh boy, did that dog—whatever his name was—jump!

But after he'd ripped through his slice, he rolled on the ground. And then the pizza...well, let's just say the pizza came out the same way it went in!

"MOM!" O'Ryan called. "We have a PROB-lem!"

"Maybe giving him a slice wasn't such a good idea," Reese said.

When Mom came into the living room and saw how the puppy had "decorated" the floor, she nodded. "Well, it's a good thing you girls are so *responsible,* because I know you'll do a good job of cleaning up the puppy's mess."

"Ugh," the girls groaned.

"Yup," Mom said, "and you'll have to clean up after him when he pees again, probably in another minute. *This* is what owning a puppy is all about."

O'Ryan and Reese looked at each other and frowned. This was not exactly what the girls had in mind when they'd been dreaming of a doggy.

"The puppy puke is starting to smell," Vanessa said, fanning her nose.

"Well, since it is a special day, I'll do the honors this time," Mom replied, pointing to the mess. "Why don't you guys go outside for a little air."

"Thanks, Mom," Reese said.

"I'll get the leash," O'Ryan said.

As the girls walked outside with the dog, Vanessa turned to the twins. "So, were you guys really surprised by the party? Or did you know?"

"No, I had no idea!" O'Ryan answered.

"Me neither. I was supremely surprised!" Reese echoed. "I mean, I can't believe all you guys kept it secret from us."

"Well," Gwen smiled, "it really wasn't that hard since Oki and I didn't know about it, either."

"You *didn't*?" O'Ryan asked, turning to Oki.

"No," Oki said, sounding ticked. "But I *wish* I had."

"Well, we just thought it'd be better to keep it between us fifth graders," Yvette replied.

Oki's mouth dropped open. She was trying to stay cool—she hadn't wanted to believe Yvette and Vanessa were being age-snobs like they'd been at lunch the other day—but it seemed like they were.

"Are you kidding?" Oki said. "What does being older have to do with anything? I mean you can be a really mature nine-year-old and a really immature eleven-year-old. It's all about the person!"

"Yeah, but we know how hard it is keeping a secret from your best friends," Vanessa tried to explain, since everyone knew that Oki was O'Ryan's BFF and Gwen was Reese's.

"So we thought we'd just make it easier for you," Yvette added.

Remembering how she'd accidentally told Reese they were going to Rinky Dink, Gwen responded, "Well, to be honest, I might not have been able to keep the surprise party all to myself."

"But you didn't even give us the chance to blow it!" Oki replied. "You just made the decision for us, without even thinking about how that might have made us feel."

Hearing the commotion, the puppy started whimpering. He seemed pretty upset, too.

As the girls tried to calm the little dog down, Yvette took a moment to think about what Oki had just said, and she realized that if she'd been in the same position, she would have felt hurt, too.

"You know what, Oki?" Yvette said. "You're right. I wasn't thinking about how it might have made you feel. I was only thinking about the surprise, which wasn't very mature of *me*, was it?"

"Not really." Oki smiled, beginning to feel better that her friend was willing to admit her mistake. "But owning up to it *is* very mature of you."

Then the friends hugged—Yvette and Oki, Vanessa and Gwen. The puppy also let it be known that he was happy with the way things had turned out. And he showed this by peeing again (just as Mom had predicted)!

"Okay, enough of all this make-up stuff!" O'Ryan said, happy that her friends were friends again. "We've got stuff to do—like getting back to the house and getting on with the party!"

"Back to the *slumber* party!" Reese said.

"Back to Eggsmerelda!" Gwen shouted. "I left her in your fridge to keep her cool. You think she'll be all right in there?"

"Sure," O'Ryan replied. "Unless Dad got hungry…"

"Hey," Vanessa said when the girls were back inside, "you guys still haven't opened your presents!"

"More presents?" Reese asked. "This party keeps getting better and better."

So the girls ran upstairs to the twins' room where the great unwrapping fiesta began!

"Cool, a zebra-striped doggy bed!" Reese said, when she opened Yvette and Vanessa's gift.

"Rockin'," O'Ryan shouted when she saw the puppy-print jammies Gwen had gotten them.

"S-weet!" Both girls giggled when they opened Oki's gift—a bright yellow doggy raincoat with four little booties.

"These gifts are so groovy, girls!" Reese said.

"Thank you, thank you!" O'Ryan added.

And then another round of hugging took place.

"I don't know about you guys," Gwen said, after all the presents had been opened, "but it was such a big day today, I'm beat like a drum."

"I'm so glad you said that!" Yvette replied. "'Cause all the secret-keeping and the party-planning wiped me out, too."

"Well, girls, this is just a *suggestion*," Vanessa said, smiling, "but maybe we want to think about getting into our PJs and going to sleep."

"Now that sounds like a very *mature* idea." Oki nodded.

"Yeah! And let's bring the puppy's crate up here so he can sleep with us, too," O'Ryan suggested.

"Good thinking," Reese said.

But as soon as the girls turned the lights out, this is what they heard:

"AAAA-RRRRRUUUUUUUWWWWW!"

"Excuse me!" Gwen giggled. "Usually, my stomach doesn't rumble that loud."

Reese turned on the light, and she saw the puppy standing at attention in his crate.

"Okay, doggy, it's *really* time for bed," O'Ryan said, patting the dog's paws. Then she flipped off the light switch.

"AAAA-RRRRRUUUUUUUWWWWW!" the dog went again. Followed by, "AAAA-RRRRUUUWWW!" and then, "AAAA-RRRRRUUUUUUUWWWWW!"

But no matter what the girls did—taking the dog out of the crate, holding and petting him, or giving him a chew toy—their new pup kept whimpering.

Funnily enough, much like the other Groovy Girls at their first sleepover, their newest (four-legged) member decided he wanted to stay awake ALL NIGHT LONG.

"Okay, doggy!" Vanessa said at 1:30 in the A.M. "Really, now it's time to lie down and go to sleep."

"AAAA-RRRRRUUUUUUUWWWWW!" the puppy howled in response.

And at 2:15 A.M., just as Yvette had started dozing off again: "AAAA-RRRRRUUUUUUUWWWW!"

By 5:17, Oki's eyes were burning from being open so long. "Puppy, what are you trying to do to us?" she asked.

But it seemed like the answer was pretty clear: He was trying to help them stay awake ALL NIGHT, just like they'd once *thought* they wanted to do.

At 8:30 A.M. when the girls finally gave up on sleeping, they trooped downstairs to get some breakfast.

"Well," O'Ryan said, "thanks to our new doggy, Groovy Girls Slumber Party Number Three turned out to be the first official No-Sleep Sleepover Party we'd ever had!"

"Yeah, thanks a lot, puppy," Gwen said, not sounding very thankful.

"Good news is," Reese nodded, "now that we've done it, we'll NEVER have to do it again!"

And all the Groovies couldn't have agreed more!

What My Egg Baby Taught Me

By: Reese McCloud

This Responsible Citizen project taught me that being responsible for something is hard. It taught me that having to take care of an egg is hard. And it taught me that when an egg hits the floor, it doesn't stay hard!...Just kidding.

But, I learned something else, too. I learned Gwen is one of the most responsible citizens I know. She not only takes great care of an egg, but she takes great care of her friends, too.

Even though she was scared of dogs, she came to the puppy farm on my birthday because she knew how much it would mean to me. And because she was willing to check it out, she learned that some dogs aren't really scary at all!

I know now that having a puppy is a lot of work. In fact, O'Ryan and I named our new puppy "Sleepless." (Did I mention that he doesn't like to sleep through the night?) Anyway, a dog needs someone who is kind, loving, and responsible. So that's why I think Gwen should get a Pearlman Puppy. Because I can't imagine any pup being doggone luckier than to get Gwen as an owner!

Groovy Girls™
sleepover handbook

SENSATIONAL SURPRISES & BIRTHDAY BASHES:
Great Ideas for **SUPER CELEBRATIONS**

3

Super-Sized Stuff
You're in for Some **BIG-TIME** Fun

Ready for a **FOUR-LEGGED FRIEND?**
Find out if you're pet-perfect

Contents

Text by Julia Marsden
Illustrations by Yancey Labat, Bill Alger, Kurt Marquart

A Groovy Greeting

HI, GROOVY GIRL!

Guess what?! The Groovies are planning a surprise sleepover party for you and your friends!

Uh-oh—I did it again!

When it comes to super-spectacular celebrations—like surprise birthday parties—I just can't seem to keep my lips sealed! Well, that's okay, because now that I let you in on our little secret, I can share with you all our totally terrific ideas, games, and delish recipes (which are great fun, whether you're celebrating a birthday or not).

Inside you'll find ways to surprise your BFF all day long.

Does she like snooping around for birthday presents (like a certain pair of twins I know)? Then turn to page 6 to plan a scavenger-hunt adventure.

Maybe you'd like to invite a few furry friends to your party! You'll be feeling the puppy love (and kitty, hamster, and birdie love, too) in no time with all kinds of purrrrr-fect pets! See pages 8–10.

And what would a party be without some yummy-licious treats?! Turn to pages 12–14 for super-duper desserts and snacks like dog-bone cookies and cupcake critters to serve at your surprise sleepover. Mmmmmm, just talking about these goodies is making me hungry! (Is it lunchtime yet?)

Now, there's only one prob—how are you going to keep all these splenderrific secrets and surprises all to yourself? Well, page 7 should give you some tips, and if you're anything like me—lots of "oops's" and "sorry's" and "I didn't really just say that's" will help, too!

See you again soon, groovy girl! And keep this just between us, okay?

Kisses and hugs,
Gwen

BRING ON THE BiRTHDAY SURPRiSES!

Planning special surprises for a friend on her birthday can be a piece of cake! Why not start by making plans for a birthday sleepover like the Groovies do? You can let everyone in on the "reason" for the get-together except the birthday girl!

🎁 After she's opened her birthday presents, create an outfit made from the gift wrap, bows, and ribbons for her to wear. Fashion a belt with ribbons and accessorize with a bow. A gift bag can make a happening handbag!

🎁 Beat the birthday girl to the bathroom in the morning and write a birthday message on the bathroom mirror using a dry-erase pen. (Be sure to get her parents' permission first!)

If your friend's birthday is during the week:

1. Give her a birthday bagel, muffin, doughnut, or cupcake with a birthday candle stuck in it when you meet up in the morning at school.

2. Give small gifts (like stickers, candy bars, or fun pencils) throughout the day that total the number of years the birthday girl will be celebrating. Or give her a homemade gift, like a batch of cookies, or a birthday coupon book (see page 11).

3. Tie balloons to her locker or desk at school.

Pooch-y Keen Party Planner

If you love animals as much as the twins do, why not unleash a party that's a real canine caper! Consider these cool ideas...

Put together a party playlist or look for a compilation CD that includes songs like:

* Who Let the Dogs Out? *Baha Men*
* You Ain't Nothing But a Hound Dog *Elvis Presley*
* (How Much Is That) Doggy in the Window *Patti Page*
* Me and You and a Dog Named Boo *Kent LaVoie*

Stage a dance contest by having guests create a dance that they teach everyone else. The guest who best "trains" the others with her dance tricks is the winner. Also, play your tunes or use them as the music that stops when you play Hot Dog (see below).

Serve tasty treats such as Pups in a Blanket (wrap hot dogs in crescent-roll dough and bake until the dough is golden), and a munchy, crunchy snack like People Chow (see page 13). Then let each guest decorate her own cute cupcake critters (see page 14).

Teach an old dog new tricks with this variation on the traditional party game below!

Hot Dog
What You Do:

Play this game—a variation of Hot Potato—by passing around a stuffed animal puppy that's wrapped in multiple layers of wrapping paper. Play some music from the pooch playlist above and, when the music stops, the girl holding the present gets to unwrap a layer of paper. Start the music again and continue passing the present. The girl who unwraps the last layer of gift wrap gets to keep the stuffed pooch.

SURPRISE-PARTY SCAVENGER HUNT

Keep the excitement going with a scavenger hunt!

* Decide on the number of players or teams and whether you're going to play inside or out (or a combo of both).

* Players will search for items on a scavenger-hunt list you make ahead of time.

* Working together or on their own, players search for the items on their lists. The items can be a combination of the stuff you hide for them to find, and easy-to-find stuff that you don't have to hide (like a multi-colored leaf or a lost button). No one should have to look through cupboards or drawers.

* Let everyone know which areas of the house or yard are considered part of the hunt area.

Here's the type of list you can make for your birthday scavenger hunt:

1. A birthday candle
2. A piece of birthday wrapping paper
3. A birthday card

* Set a time limit.

* Award prizes to the person or team who finds everything on the list the fastest.

* For a birthday-themed scavenger hunt, you can also write the words "HAPPY BIRTHDAY" or the birthday girl's name vertically down one side of a piece of paper. Then list objects that start with each letter that can be found in the area where the party is taking place. Here's an example using Reese's and O'Ryan's names.

Red crayon
Earring
Eraser
Spoon
Envelope

Oven mitt
Rubber band
Yarn
Apple
Nail file

Super-Secret Tips and Pet-Perfect Solutions

If you've got a secret that's too good to keep to yourself, or a secret wish for a pet of your own...read on! These helpful tips are made for you.

Pssst! I've Got a Secret!

My friends and I are planning a surprise birthday party for my BFF, but I'm finding it really hard to keep it a secret from her. I always feel like I'm about to spill the beans. What should I do?

It totally makes sense that you're having a tough time keeping this exciting info to yourself. After all, you and your BFF are probably used to sharing all kinds of secrets. When you feel like you're about to tell all, steer your conversation toward a sharable secret that you're both already in on. And if you're on the phone with her, stage a quick wrap-up of your talk and speed dial one of your friends who's in on the party planning. The two of you will be able to talk about the upcoming bash all you want without blowing the surprise.

Puppy Love

I really want a puppy. My parents keep telling me that having a pet is a lot of work. How can I prove to them that I'm ready for the responsibility?

There's way more to having a dog than feeding it treats and showing it off to your friends. As a responsible canine caretaker, your daily duties are going to include things such as feeding, walking, and grooming your pooch. Why not offer to take care of a neighbor's pet for a few days to show your parents how committed you are to caring for an animal of your own? Or let your parents know that you'll be taking care of an egg baby, sugar baby, or flour baby (a practice substitute for the real thing you'll be responsible for) for a week or more. Your actions are likely to go a long way toward showing them how responsible you can be when it comes to caring for a pet.

ANIMAL ANTICS

The Right Pet for You

Picking a pet can be both super-fun and exciting, but also a big responsibility! Want to know what pet might be right for you? Check out this info and see if you can make yourself a pet-perfect match!

Dogs

A dog can be a girl's best friend! Because canines can offer unconditional love and loyalty, it's easy to fall in love! Your pooch will be there for you as you leave for school each morning, and it'll be waiting happily for you at your doorstep when you return. Your pet will cuddle up next to you when you're sad, and listen to all you have to say. But with all this doggy love comes hard work and responsibility. Dogs need plenty of attention and time out—outside that is, for walks and exercise. For more about dog care and a list of some kid-friendly pooches, turn to page 10.

Overall care level: *High*

Cats

If you're looking for a cuddly companion who's also independent and less time-consuming than a dog (they don't need to be walked, after all!), then a cat may be the purrrrr-fect pet for you! Unlike dogs, cats don't need to be brought outside when they have to go to the bathroom—they have a litter box indoors instead. And because they groom themselves so well, you won't need to comb their fur as much as a dog's, and you don't need to take them to the groomer's for a bath and haircut!

Overall care level: *Medium to high*

Birds

Some pets are for the birds! If you'd like a chirpy, feathered friend, who prefers a splash to a comb-out— then maybe a pet bird is for you! Cockatiels have very sweet personalities and soft voices. You can even teach them to speak a few words! Parakeets and finches like to be kept in pairs—so they're good at keeping themselves company. And if music is your thing, then a male canary is the right birdie match for you! When they're happy, they can sing beautiful melodies. **Overall care level:** *Medium*

Fish

Goldfish make a great first pet. They're pretty easy to take care of, and not very time-consuming. After all, they don't need to be cuddled, held, or taken outside for a walk! You'll need a fishbowl, which needs to be cleaned about once a week, and some fish food (it's important not to overfeed your fish—a pinch a day should do the trick!). Overall care level: *Low*

Hamsters

To keep a hamster happy, you need a cage (which should be cleaned once a week), a hamster wheel for exercise, a wooden chew toy so they won't gnaw on the cage bars (hamsters have small but sharp teeth!), a water bottle, and some hamster-mix food. While hamsters are furry, cute, and totally fun to play with, they're often up at night because they're nocturnal (which means they sleep during the day). So, unless you want to drift off to sleep to the sound of a squeaky hamster wheel, it's best to keep your furry friend in a room other than your bedroom. Other little pets that are in the same category as hamsters are mice, gerbils, and guinea pigs. **Overall care level:** *Medium*

BEST OF THE BREEDS

So, you're ready for a pooch pal and can't wait for the bark-o-rama fest to begin! What kind of dog should you get? Read on for facts and tips about finding the perfect canine companion for you and your family!

Big or Small—They're All Super-Duper Dogs!

Will you pick a pizzaz-zy big dog or a sensational small one? Big dogs (like golden retrievers and Labrador retrievers) need lots of room. If your home doesn't have a lot of open space, or your pet won't be given the run of the house, then you may want to choose a smaller dog (like a bichon frise or toy poodle).

Kid-friendly Canines

- If you'd like a kid-friendly gentle giant, consider: golden retrievers and Labrador retrievers.

- If you'd like a kid-friendly petite pooch, consider: pugs, toy poodles, and bichon frises.

- If you'd like a kid-friendly super-smart dog, consider: border collies and poodles.

- If you'd like a kid-friendly dog for the country, consider: spaniels, golden retrievers, and Labradors.

- If you'd like a kid-friendly dog for the city, consider: pugs and Boston terriers.

- If you want to give a home to a one-of-a-kind dog, consider a mixed-breed (mutt). Each dog has its own personality, but many mutts are very kid-friendly.

Eggs-tra Credit

While waiting for permission for a pup, try taking care of an egg baby!

To make an egg baby of your own, use colored markers to draw a face on an uncooked egg. For an added touch, glue some yarn on the top of the egg for hair.

To make a sugar or flour baby, decorate a plain piece of paper with a face, and then wrap the paper around a 5-pound bag of sugar or flour and tape it in place. To really doll things up, fit your sack with a small baby or doll outfit. Then top things off with a small baby bonnet!

A Fun-Filled Gift to Make for a
FRiEND'S BiRTHDAY

Birthday Coupon Book

Your friend's birthday is coming up and you want to make her something that's one-of-a-kind special. Create a coupon book that the birthday girl can turn in to you at anytime, page by page, for all kinds of fun!

What You Do:

1. Trace the outline of your coupon on colored construction paper or card stock using a dollar bill as your guide. Make as many pages for your book as you like—a pack of ten coupons makes a great gift!

2. Write out and decorate individual coupons that say what they can be redeemed—or traded in—for.
Some coupons can be for small treats, while others can be for things that are truly priceless, or unique to your special friendship.

3. Once you've made all of the individual coupons, create a cover and a message page that says something like: *This birthday coupon book is my way of wishing you a happy birthday. These coupons never expire and can be redeemed at any time.*

What You Need:

* Card stock or construction paper
* Colored pens or markers
* Stickers (optional)
* Stapler

Here are some examples:

* A Manicure by Me in the Color of Your Choice
* Ice-Cream Run! A Double Scoop Ice-Cream Cone— My Treat!
* An Hour of Help with Your Chores
* Fabulous Free Phone Advice— All You Have to Do Is Call!
* A Batch of Homemade Cookies
* A Great Big Hug
* A Shoulder to Lean On

BONE APPETIT

If you're as much of a dog lover as Reese and O'Ryan, then you'll want to whip up these winning recipes for some delightful doggy-themed birthday desserts and snacks!

Doggone Delicious Sugar Cookies

Like the Groovy Girls, you probably know how sweet it can be to have a pup to play with. But when the munchies strike, throw a dog a bone and pick up one of these sweet treats for yourself!

Dog-Bone Cookies

(Makes about 3 dozen cookies)

Ingredients:

- $1/2$ cup butter, softened
- 1 cup white sugar
- 2 eggs
- 1 teaspoon vanilla extract
- $2^1/2$ cups all-purpose flour
- 1 teaspoon baking powder
- $1/2$ teaspoon salt
- Rainbow sprinkles

Utensils: Measuring cups, measuring spoons, large mixing bowl, mixer, foil or plastic wrap, spatula, rolling pin, butter knife, cookie sheet

What else you need: A grown-up to help you

What You Do:

1. In a large mixing bowl, use a mixer to cream together the softened butter and sugar until smooth. Beat in the eggs and vanilla. By hand, stir in the flour, baking powder, and salt. Cover the bowl and chill in the fridge for at least one hour or overnight.

2. Have an adult preheat the oven to 400 degrees F. Roll out the dough on a floured surface so it's $1/4$- to $1/2$-inch thick. Cut into dog-bone shapes using your Dog Bone Cookie Cut-Out (see page 13) and a butter knife.

3. Decorate with sprinkles. Place the cookies one inch apart on an un-greased cookie sheet.

4. Have an adult place the cookie sheet in the preheated oven and bake the cookies for about 7 minutes. Cool completely.

Dog Bone Cookie Cut-Out

What You Need:

- Paper
- Pencil
- Tape
- A small piece of cardboard or card stock
- Scissors

What You Do:

1. On a piece of paper, trace the dotted dog-bone outline at the top of the opposite page.

2. Cut out the dog-bone shape and tape it to the cardboard or card stock.

3. Cut out the dog-bone shape again, this time from the cardboard, and use this pattern and a butter knife to cut out your dog-bone cookies from the cookie dough. Or, you can use a dog-bone-shaped cookie cutter from a cooking supplies or crafts store.

People Chow *(Makes about 5 cups)*

Kibble is cool for canines, but this crunchy snack is sure to please the people in your life!

Ingredients:

1 cup Corn Chex® cereal
1 cup Rice Chex® cereal
1 cup Wheat Chex® cereal
1 cup peanuts or your favorite nut
$^1/_2$ cup raisins
Utensils: Measuring cups, spoon, large mixing bowl

What You Do:

1. Mix all ingredients together in a large mixing bowl.

2. Store in an airtight container or serve to your guests in personalized plastic dog bowls.

* Surprise Party People Chow!

You provide the peanuts and raisins. Then ask each of your party guests to bring one cup of her favorite unsweetened cereal in a zip-top plastic sandwich bag. When guests arrive, have them add what they brought to a large mixing bowl. Stir it up and then serve the snack that now has several surprise ingredients!

CUPCAKE CRITTERS

Give a plain cupcake a surprising finish with decorating details that turn an ordinary treat into something with animal appeal!

Lovable Lab

What You Need:

Chocolate frosting

Shredded coconut

Black shoestring licorice or black decorating icing

Small candies such as mini M&M's® or jelly beans, red fruit leather, or red decorating icing

What You Do:

Frost a cupcake with chocolate frosting. (Mix some shredded coconut into the frosting to create a furry coat.) Use black licorice string pieces or black decorating icing to create two floppy ears and mouth. Use small candies to create eyes and a nose. Flatten and curl a small piece of red fruit leather, or use red decorating icing, to create a tongue.

Cool Cat

What You Need:

* Frosting in your color of choice
* Small candies
* Black shoestring licorice
* Sugar wafer cookies or graham crackers

What You Do:

Frost a cupcake, and add small candies for eyes and a nose. Place short pieces of shoestring licorice near the nose for whiskers. Use a butter knife to cut a sugar wafer cookie or graham cracker into two small triangular pieces for ears. Add to the cupcake, and frost.

Funny Bunny

What You Need:

* Frosting in your color of choice
* Two peanut-shaped cookies such as Nutter Butters®
* Small candies

What You Do:

Frost a cupcake. Place two peanut-shaped cookies at the top of the cupcake to form rabbit ears. Frost the tops and sides of the cookies to match the rabbit face. Add eyes and a nose using small candies. Then make whiskers like you did for the cat.

Strange and Silly
SUPER-SIZED Stuff!

If you took a road trip out to Large Lou's Museum of Loo-Loos—just like the Groovy Girls do—you would find a bunch of crazy creations. Here are some fun ones you can make yourself!

Clip Art Jump Rope

What You Need:

- Multi-colored plastic-coated paper clips

What You Do:

Hook the paper clips together, making a paper clip chain long enough to use as a jump rope. Then get hopping! Or clip the two ends together to make an awesome accessory—a necklace that you can wrap around several times over!

Big Rubber-Band Ball

-What You Need:

- Lots of rubber bands, both small and large

What You Do:

1. Tie a large rubber band into several knots.

2. Wrap a small rubber band around the large rubber band wad to create the core of your ball. You may have to wrap one rubber band around the core several times.

3. Continue adding small rubber bands.

4. When the small rubber bands will no longer stretch around the ball, switch to the larger rubber bands. When these larger rubber bands can no longer make it around the ball, tie two rubber bands together and then stretch them around. Whenever you and your friends are together, add to your creation.

Angel Wings 3-Books-in-1!

Read all the Angel Wings adventures:

New Friends
Birthday Surprise
Secrets and Sapphires

And coming soon:
Rainbows and Halos

ANGEL WINGS

Angel Wings 3-Books-in-1!

New Friends

Birthday Surprise

Secrets and Sapphires

by MICHELLE MISRA

illustrated by SAMANTHA CHAFFEY

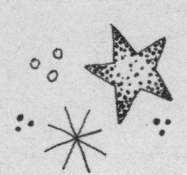

ALADDIN

New York London Toronto Sydney New Delhi

ALADDIN

An imprint of Simon & Schuster Children's Publishing Division
1230 Avenue of the Americas, New York, NY 10020
This Aladdin paperback edition November 2016
New Friends text copyright © 2013 by Michelle Misra and Linda Chapman
New Friends interior illustrations copyright © 2013 by Samantha Chaffey
Birthday Surprise text copyright © 2012 by Michelle Misra and Linda Chapman
Birthday Surprise interior illustrations copyright © 2012 by Samantha Chaffey
Secrets and Sapphires text copyright © 2013 by Michelle Misra and Linda Chapman
Secrets and Sapphires interior illustrations copyright © 2013 by Samantha Chaffey
Cover illustrations copyright © 2016 by Christina Forshay
All rights reserved, including the right of reproduction in whole or in part in any form.
ALADDIN and related logo are registered trademarks of Simon & Schuster, Inc.
For information about special discounts for bulk purchases, please contact
Simon & Schuster Special Sales at 1-866-506-1949 or business@simonandschuster.com.
The Simon & Schuster Speakers Bureau can bring authors to your live event.
For more information or to book an event contact the Simon & Schuster Speakers Bureau
at 1-866-248-3049 or visit our website at www.simonspeakers.com.
Designed by Karina Granda
The text of this book was set in Bembo STD.
Manufactured in the United States of America 1016 OFF
2 4 6 8 10 9 7 5 3 1
Library of Congress Control Number 2016951740
ISBN 978-1-4814-8567-8
ISBN 978-1-4814-5799-6 (*New Friends* eBook)
ISBN 978-1-4814-5802-3 (*Birthday Surprise* eBook)
ISBN 978-1-4814-5805-4 (*Secrets and Sapphires* eBook)
These titles were previously published individually by Aladdin.

CONTENTS

New Friends

For Emily Mullen,
a very special girl

CHAPTER 1

A New School

OH, WOW!" ELLA BROWN BREATHED as she looked through the big golden gates. On the other side of them was a castle made of pure glass. It sparkled like a diamond in the sunshine. Ella's wings fluttered. The Guardian Angel Academy. It was just how she had always imagined it would be—totally perfect!

Ella checked her reflection in the shining gates. Her white halo was sitting straight, her brown, shoulder-length hair was glossy, and her green eyes sparkled. She couldn't wait to start her very first day!

She reached for the bell, but before she could press it, the gates swung open. A long driveway led to the castle entrance, parting fields of wild flowers. Bright butterflies flew from flower to flower and the gentle sound of bees hummed in the air.

Angel-tastic! This was going to be so much fun! Ella half skipped and half flew forward, her tiny wings fluttering as they carried her along the driveway. There were bound to be lots of adventures in store at angel school. She flew up and pirouetted at the thought.

"Okay, so how *do* you do that?"

Ella spun around to see a very tall girl, about

her own age, behind her. The girl was dressed in the same pearly white uniform as Ella but she didn't look like your average neat and tidy angel. Her dress already had dirty splotches on it and a tangle of blonde curls was scrambling out from under her halo.

"Do what?" Ella asked, surprised.

"Make your wings work like that!" The girl peered over her shoulder at her own wings. "I've been trying to make mine work ever since they appeared, but they just don't seem to. Look!" She jumped up in the air. Her wings gave a few faint flaps but didn't manage to lift her up. "Oh, I'm useless!"

"No you're not. It just takes practice," Ella told her. "I just think fluttery thoughts. Imagine you're a butterfly, swooping and gliding. . . ."

Ella was picturing it so clearly that her own wings fluttered and she rose into the air. "Like that!" she giggled, floating down again.

The tall girl concentrated hard. "Okay, here goes. I'm imagining, I'm imagining . . ."

"Keep on trying. You can do it!" Ella encouraged. The other girl's wings started to flutter faster and suddenly she shot up into the sky like a rocket.

"Whoa!" she cried in alarm, turning a loop-the-loop and coming down again, her arms flailing. She would have crashed to the ground but Ella rushed forward to catch her just in time.

"Thank you!" gasped the other girl. A grin lit up her face. "Hey, I flew! I really flew! I might not have won any points for style, but I did it—and it felt totally awesome." She hugged Ella, almost knocking her over. "So what's your name? I'm Poppy."

"I'm Ella," Ella replied.

"And is it your first day too?" Poppy asked. Ella nodded.

"Can we be friends?" Poppy said, giving her a hopeful look.

"Well . . ." Ella paused teasingly. "Do you like adventures?"

"Oh yes!" breathed Poppy.

Ella broke into a smile. "Then we can be best friends!"

Poppy grinned. "That's totally *cherub-azing*!"

Ella linked arms with her and looked up at the glittering castle. "Look out, Guardian Angel Academy. Here we come!"

CHAPTER 2

Crash Landing!

ELLA AND POPPY HURRIED DOWN the driveway. On one side there was a mysterious forest of tall green trees. "You know, we could always go and do a little exploring," Ella said.

"Okay," Poppy said, eagerly. They set off toward the trees.

"Where are you two going?" a shrill voice exclaimed from behind them.

They swung around. Another angel about

their age was flying down the driveway. She looked absolutely perfect, her golden hair was curled into ringlets, and her white uniform was spotless. "Were you about to go in the woods?"

"Possibly," Ella replied cautiously.

The blonde angel folded her arms. "The school rules say we should go straight to school. Don't you know angels should never break rules?" She stuck her nose in the air. "Mommy was right. She said that I would probably meet some badly brought-up angels when I got here."

"That's a horrible thing to say!" Poppy protested.

The blonde angel looked her up and down. "Halos and wings, look at you! Were you dragged through a bush on your way here? Haven't you read the school handbook?" She pulled a book out from the pocket in her uniform and smugly read out. "For your information: *Angels should strive to be neat and tidy at all times.* That's what it says here on page one. Along with: *Angels should always obey school rules."* She gave Ella a pointed look, and tossing her ringlets back, she flew on her way.

"I think *she* must have missed the page that says angels should be kind and polite at all times." Ella exclaimed.

Poppy giggled. "I suppose she is right, though, and we probably shouldn't break the rules on our very first day!"

They headed after the snooty angel. Getting closer to the castle, they saw that there were angels everywhere. Most of them were older than Ella and Poppy and were flying effortlessly.

"Isn't the castle massive?" sighed Poppy, looking up at the glittering turrets. Craning her head, she tripped over a stone and promptly fell over.

"Oh my goodness, are you all right?" An older angel flew over as Ella helped Poppy up.

"I'm guessing you must be Poppy and Ella," she said. "I've been looking out for you. My name is Seraphina. I'm a Guardian Angel and a teacher here."

"I like your halo." Ella gazed at Seraphina's glittering diamond halo.

"Thank you." Seraphina looked pleased. "It hasn't always been so special. When you start at the Academy you have a white halo, but they change as you prove what a good angel you are."

Ella knew that. White became sapphire, sapphire became ruby, ruby became emerald, and so on, until eventually gold became diamond. It was the same with the uniform—that changed color too, and your wings grew bigger and more downy and feathery with each change in halo color. If you had a diamond halo by the end of your seven years at the Academy you would become a Guardian Angel when you graduated, and then you could be a teacher or go to the human world and protect people.

"I finished at the Academy last term," said Seraphina, her wings glowing as they changed with every color of the rainbow. "And now I'm going to be the tutor for the new third graders, so you'll be seeing quite a lot of me! Now, come with me and I'll show you around."

She led them through the big front door. Ella and Poppy both gasped as they looked around the huge hall. White fluffy clouds bobbed about and, through them, they could see a ceiling covered with iridescent moons and stars. It was set against a dark background, making it look like the most magical starry

night ever. Chandeliers hung down and a spiral staircase led upward in the center of the room.

"It's wonderful," whispered Poppy.

"Totally glittery!" said Ella.

"It is rather amazing, isn't it?" Seraphina agreed. Another angel with a diamond halo passed by with three young angels following her. She smiled at the girls and said hello to Seraphina before guiding her girls up the staircase. "That's Angel Celestine, she teaches Angel Gardening," said Seraphina.

"You both have beautiful names," Poppy said.

"They're your angel names, aren't they?" said Ella.

Seraphina nodded. "I can see you've been reading your handbook, Ella. Excellent!"

Ella blushed. Despite what the angel in the

driveway had said, she did in fact know the handbook by heart. It had all the basic angel rules in it. When angels finished at the Academy and became Guardian Angels, they were also given a special angel name. She wondered what hers would be—if she ever got to be a Guardian Angel that is!

"Now let me show you to your dorm." Seraphina led them up the spiral staircase. On the first floor there was a circular hall where assemblies were held and the dining hall where they would eat their meals. On the second floor there was a maze of different classrooms. On the third floor there were six hallways leading away from the spiral staircase into different turrets. "The third-grade dorms are down there." Seraphina pointed to a nearby hallway with planets all over the walls and ceiling. "We could fly to your dorm if you like."

"Great!" exclaimed Ella.

"Er, okay," Poppy said doubtfully.

Ella screwed her face up in concentration. Her wings started to beat and she flew into the hallway.

"Not too fast now, Ella!" called Seraphina.

But Ella just couldn't help herself. She wanted to impress Seraphina and she was enjoying the feeling of the wind rushing past her. Flying was easy! She went faster and faster, thinking how angel-tastic she must look. Yippee!

"Ella! Please slow down!" Seraphina cried anxiously.

"I'm fine!" Ella called. "I really am!" But just then, the door of one the dorms opened and two angels came out. There was nothing Ella could do.

"Whoa!" she yelled as she collided with them.

Crash!

All three angels landed in a tangled heap on the floor!

CHAPTER 3

Magical Dorms

'M SORRY!" ELLA GASPED. ONE OF THE angels had red, shoulder-length hair and a disdainful expression. The other angel was blonde. "Not you again!" she snapped at Ella.

Ella groaned inwardly. Oh no. Of all the angels in the school, she'd gone and crashed into the angel they had met earlier.

Ella hastily held out her hand. "I really am sorry. Here, let me help you up."

The blonde angel ignored her hand and

snorted. "I'd much rather you helped me by staying out of my way! *Completely* out of it!" She scrambled to her feet. Her halo was now sitting crookedly on her head and there was a smudge of dirt on her face.

Seraphina landed beside them.

"Come along now, Primrose. I know you're upset, but Ella *has* just apologized to you."

All traces of anger vanished from Primrose's face as she saw the teacher. "I'm sorry, Angel Seraphina," she said, blinking her eyes. "It was just such an awful shock and I was ever so worried in case my new friend, Veronica, had been hurt in any way." She looked at the redheaded angel with a sweet and caring expression.

Seraphina nodded kindly. "I understand, my dear. Now back into your dorm please."

Primrose and Veronica went back into their dorm. Seraphina turned and looked at Ella. Ella bit her lip, expecting to see anger in the teacher's eyes, but there was only a look of sadness. Somehow that made her feel even worse.

"Ella, why did you ignore me?" Seraphina said softly. "I asked you to slow down."

"I know. I'm sorry." Ella hung her head.

"I was just so excited with it being the first day and, well, I suppose I was showing off a bit," she admitted. "It was really stupid of me, Angel Seraphina. I am really very sorry." She swallowed.

There was a pause. "That is very honest of you," Seraphina said. "And honesty is a good quality for an angel to have. You know, I think we will say no more about it. However, in the future, you really must do as you're told or you'll never become a Guardian Angel. Now"—Seraphina's tone changed—"why don't you and Poppy come and meet your dorm-mates?" Ella looked up and saw two other angels looking out of a door at the end of the hallway. One had light brown hair and a dreamy expression,

and the other was small with a long, dark ponytail and looked sporty. She and Poppy followed Seraphina over.

"This is Tilly," Seraphina said, nodding at the girl with the light brown hair.

"And I'm Jessica, but call me Jess," said the smaller girl, smiling.

"I'll leave you four to get to know one another," said Seraphina. "See you at dinnertime." And with that, she flew away.

"Well, that certainly was some arrival!" said Tilly, grinning at Ella.

"Crashing into Primrose of all people, too," said Jess, her brown eyes wide.

"Forget about it now," Tilly told Ella. "Come into our dorm!"

Going inside, Ella gasped. There was a large

oval window looking out over the grounds, as well as four white closets and four dressing tables, each with one of their names in large golden letters. A statue of a golden dove on a perch swung from the ceiling high above their heads. But it wasn't those things that made Ella gasp most. She was staring at the beds. They looked like floating clouds, but with comforters and pillows on them! One was rose-pink, one lilac, one aquamarine, and one pale green.

"Cupid's arrow!" said Ella, as the clouds jostled around the room.

"They're the comfiest things ever," said Tilly, scrambling onto the aquamarine cloud. "The lilac is yours, Ella, and the pink one is Poppy's."

Ella and Poppy ran to their clouds. Poppy hesitated for a moment.

"Don't worry," Jess said, seeing her face. "I was worried too at first, but tell yourself you won't fall through and you won't. Just jump on!"

Ella jumped on. She squealed as she sank into it. It was the softest, most wonderful bed ever!

"You can make them move around by flapping your wings," said Tilly. "We can play tag!"

Soon all four of them were zipping around, giggling as they chased one another. Ella thought it was fantastic! They finally stopped, panting and happy.

"Our dorm is definitely the best!" declared Ella in delight.

"The very best!" The other three grinned.

CHAPTER 4

Exciting News

FTER ABOUT FIFTEEN MINUTES, THE golden dove opened its mouth and started to coo.

"That means it's dinnertime!" said Jess. "It's cloudberry leaves and golden pie tonight!"

"Yum! My favorite!" said Ella.

"We always have starflower salad for dinner on Mondays at home," said Tilly, rather sadly.

"I don't care what we have for dinner, just

so long as we eat!" said Poppy. "I'm starving. Come on!"

They all ran downstairs. There were angels everywhere! The youngest angels were easily spotted because of their white dresses and halos, and smaller wings.

There were four long tables in the dining hall for the students, each loaded up with silver platters of the most delicious-looking food, and another table for the teachers. A plump angel with very wise eyes, enormous gossamer wings, and dark hair coiled in a bun was sitting at the head of the table.

"That's Archangel Grace," whispered Jess.

Ella looked over in awe at the head teacher of the Guardian Angel Academy. Archangels

were the most important angels you could get. She'd heard so many amazing stories of the good deeds Archangel Grace had performed as a Guardian Angel in the human world. It must be incredible to be a Guardian Angel and have lots of adventures.

"I wonder where we should sit . . . ," Tilly said.

Poppy headed for a table, but Ella grabbed her arm. "Not there!" Farther along the table,

Primrose and Veronica were sitting down. Primrose's hands were crossed neatly on the table, her face looking angelic. But as she caught sight of Ella and Poppy, she scowled.

Quickly, Ella turned away. Finding seats at a different table, they sat down.

There was a loud chime of bells and everyone started eating.

Ella had never had such a feast. Just when

she thought she couldn't manage another thing, massive bowls of the creamiest ice cream appeared on each table.

She was just finishing her bowl when Archangel Grace stood up.

"Greetings, my angels," she announced in a silvery voice. "Once again it is the start of a new term here at the Guardian Angel Academy. Please will you all welcome the new third graders." Everyone around the room burst into applause. Archangel Grace eventually held up her hand for silence. "And at the end of this week there will be a special start-of-term garden party for all angels who have earned at least one halo stamp."

"Hooray!" the angels cheered.

"What are halo stamps?" Poppy whispered to the others.

Ella knew, but didn't want to speak while Archangel Grace was talking. Luckily, the head teacher went on to explain. "For the benefit of our new students who may not have read the handbook completely, all students have a halo card." As she spoke, golden nightingales fluttered in and dropped a card in front of each of the new students.

Ella picked hers up. It seemed to be just a normal card.

"Every time you do something good—either in work or for behavior—you get a stamp on your halo card," Archangel Grace explained. "When the card is completely filled, your halo will change color and your wings grow a little bigger. Be warned though"—Archangel Grace's face became serious—"halo stamps can also be removed for breaking the rules or not behaving in an angelic way. But now let us turn our minds to happier things. Enjoy this evening, angels, and tomorrow your first lessons will begin!"

She sat down and everyone started to talk. "I wonder what our first lesson will be?" said Poppy.

"It's flying!" said Ella, who'd read the timetable in the handbook.

"Awesome!" exclaimed Tilly. "We're going to have to get really good at that if we're going to become Guardian Angels one day!"

There was a snort behind her. Ella turned. Primrose and Veronica were standing there.

"Guardian Angels!" Primrose said scornfully. "You four are never going to make Guardian Angels! You might as well just leave now!"

Sticking her nose in the air, Primrose linked arms with Veronica and flew away.

Ella opened her mouth, but just in time saw Seraphina watching them and bit back her sharp retort. She really couldn't get into trouble again. "Primrose is so annoying!" she hissed to her friends.

"Forget about her. Think of nice things," Jess advised. "Like our flying lesson tomorrow."

"And the start-of-term garden party!" put in Poppy.

"*If* we all have a halo stamp," Tilly added anxiously. "What if we don't?"

Ella quickly forgot Primrose. "We will!" she declared. "We'll all be at that party and we're all going to have some fun this week, just wait and see!"

CHAPTER 5

Holographic Halos!

WHEN ELLA WOKE THE NEXT MORNing, for a moment she couldn't remember where she was. But then, when she saw the golden light streaming through the window and felt the comfy cloud beneath her, she knew *exactly* where she was. The Guardian Angel Academy!

"Whoa!" she grinned, as her cloud started shifting beneath her. She quickly flapped her wings until her cloud moved downward and her feet touched the ground.

"Good night?" Jess asked, as she stretched and yawned, her eyes cloudy with sleep.

"The best!" grinned Ella.

"I was dreaming about home," said Tilly. For a moment she looked sad. "It's lovely here, but I do miss my family," she sighed.

"There's no time for missing anyone now," Poppy said cheerfully, pointing at the golden dove as it let out a morning greeting. "It's time we got up and got dressed or we'll be late for breakfast!"

The four girls scrambled out of bed.

It was very busy in the dining hall. There was everything you could possibly want for breakfast—sparkly muffins, towers of toast, the creamiest oatmeal, and juices in every color of the rainbow. Once Ella had finished, she picked up her bowl and went over to where an older angel with ruby-colored wings was carefully stacking a cart and muttering under her breath.

"Nearly dropped it . . . not another," she groaned.

"Let me help you with that," offered Ella.

"Oh you *are* an angel!" The older angel smiled, laughing at her own joke. "Thanks. My name's Holly by the way."

"And I'm Ella," said Ella.

Ella and Holly worked happily alongside each other, with one collecting and the other stacking. As Ella piled up another bowl, a voice came from behind her.

"It's not every day a new angel helps out without even being asked."

Ella spun around. "Archangel Grace!"

"I think you've earned yourself a halo stamp!" Archangel Grace beamed. "Come to my office to collect it."

A halo stamp? Ella couldn't believe her luck. "Thank you," she said excitedly as the head teacher disappeared. She couldn't wait to get it and tell the others!

"Go on," said Holly, seeming to read her mind. "Go and get your stamp. I can finish up here."

"Sure?" asked Ella.

"Positive," said Holly.

Quickly, Ella made her way out of the dining hall and up to the hallway where the Archangel's office was. She stopped outside, nervously fingering her halo card. One . . . two . . . three. Ella knocked on the door.

"Come in!" called Archangel Grace.

Ella was lost for words as she looked around the Archangel's office. It was just amazing! Little golden bells of all shapes and sizes were hanging from the ceiling, and as a breeze fluttered through an open window, they chimed musically. Archangel Grace smiled from behind her glass desk, a large book spread out before her, little half-moon glasses perched on the end of her nose.

"What's that?" Ella asked curiously, pointing at the book.

"This?" Archangel Grace smiled. "It's a map book of the whole of Angel World, my dear. Take a look, if you like."

Ella stepped forward to look at the beautiful pages. Even upside down, she could see bubbling brooks and fields of poppies. As Archangel Grace turned the page, the hum of bees and butterflies sounded around the room.

"It makes a noise." Ella jumped back, surprised.

Archangel Grace chuckled to herself. "That, my dear, is the beauty of angel magic. Now, your halo stamp. Have you got your card?"

Ella nodded and held it out.

She watched closely as Archangel Grace

took out a little pot of glittery powder from her pocket.

"Angel dust," Archangel Grace explained, sprinkling a pinch over Ella's card.

Poof! The most beautiful holographic stamp appeared on the card; it shone like silver. Ella felt a warm glow flood through her and felt

as if her own real halo was glittering more brightly too.

"Wow!" she breathed.

"Your first halo stamp is very precious," Archangel Grace said seriously. "I can still remember mine. Now, off you go—you've got flying class, haven't you?"

"I have. And thank you again, Archangel Grace," breathed Ella.

As Ella closed the door behind her, she looked again at the little stamp shimmering and sparkling on the card. It was just perfect! She felt she could have stood looking at it all day, but just then the bell rang. Ella jumped. Quick! It was time for flying class and she didn't want to be late. . . .

CHAPTER 6

High in the Sky!

NOW, ANGELS, REMEMBER YOU DON'T need to move too much to raise yourselves off the ground. Just fill your head with floaty thoughts. Gently, gently . . . ," Raffaella, the flying teacher, called out. "And remember, don't go too high or too near the trees!"

Ella closed her eyes and tried to remember everything she'd been taught. "Breathe and imagine," she muttered under her breath, filling her head with thoughts of butterflies and bees.

To her delight, her feet began to lift off the ground. She was flying!

"How are you doing, Ella?" Poppy giggled, her arms flailing as she came over. "I'm doing loads better than yesterday. Whoa!" she cried, as she lost control and spun around. In a moment, the two girls had crashed, before collapsing in a heap on the ground. But Ella didn't mind and in no time at all they were back in the air again.

"That's it, girls, keep up the good work," Raffaella encouraged. "You'll soon be flying well. Now remember, please, no flying out of the school grounds while you're third graders."

"Not at all, Angel Raffaella? But I wanted to go to Rainbow's End," said Primrose, swooping over.

"I'm afraid that is completely out of bounds, Primrose." Raffaella looked serious.

"In that case, of course I won't go there," said Primrose meekly.

"What's Rainbow's End?" Ella asked her friends.

"It's a really magical place," Tilly explained. "You can only reach it by using a rainbow near the school. It's supposed to be the most beautiful place ever."

"That's right, Ella," Raffaella said, overhearing. "Not only is Rainbow's End a very beautiful place, but a very special flower grows there—the remembering flower. It's purple, and when someone touches it, it makes them feel happy."

"How does it do that?" asked Ella.

"Ah, that is the subject of another lesson," said Raffaella with a smile. "You'll find out all about the remembering flower when you learn about magical plants. But this is a flying class. It's flying time, angels!"

Once Raffaella had moved on to help some of the others, Poppy flew back to Ella and nudged her. "So did you get your stamp?"

Ella had been longing to let the others see

her card with its stamp, but hadn't wanted to show off. "Yes," she admitted.

Primrose was still hovering near them. She snorted. "The Archangel must be crazy to give you a halo stamp, Ella Brown!"

Ella ignored her.

"Let's see it, then," said Tilly.

Ella held out her halo card.

"Wow!" Poppy breathed as she stared at the beautiful stamp. "Our dorm's first halo stamp!"

Ella grinned. "We'll all have one soon. I bet we will."

"As if!" Primrose said. Suddenly she dived forward, grabbed Ella's card, and flew off!

"Hey!" Ella cried indignantly. "Come back!"

Primrose hovered in the air. "If you want it—come and get it!" She flew higher.

"Don't, Ella," said Jess. "She'll soon get bored and come down."

But Ella flung herself into the air.

"Ella!" Poppy exclaimed. "Don't!"

Ella didn't listen. She chased after Primrose. They went higher and higher toward the tree-tops. It took a few moments before Raffaella noticed what they were doing.

"Come back here, you two!" she cried, but both Ella and Primrose were too far away to hear her. Primrose was flying as fast as she could, but Ella was gaining on her. Whizzing forward, Ella grabbed at her card.

"*Arrgh!*" Primrose called as, caught off-balance, she fell into one of the trees. Her gown and wings caught on the branches there, and, for a moment, she dangled from it like a

piece of laundry. She shrieked and struggled.

Ella looked at her in alarm. "Stay still! I'll help you."

"Get away from me!" Primrose screamed at her as the angels below all noticed and started to laugh and point.

Raffaella was already racing up to the trees. Within seconds she had reached the two girls and was untangling Primrose from the branches. Then she brought them back down to land.

"What in heaven did you think you were doing?" she exclaimed. "Didn't you hear me tell you not to fly too close to the trees? Look at you—your white dresses have got dirt all over them and the arms of them are ripped."

Primrose let out a loud wail as she looked

down at her ruined clothes. "This is all your fault," she said accusingly to Ella.

"My fault!" Ella was indignant. "You're the one who took my card and—"

"Enough!" Raffaella held up her hand. "This is both of your faults. And so I'm *de*-awarding you one halo stamp each."

"*De*-awarding?" For a moment Ella couldn't think what Raffaella meant, but after a second it started to sink in. She was taking a halo stamp away! Ella gaped. That was so unfair! She couldn't lose her precious halo stamp.

Primrose hung her head. "I haven't got a halo stamp to lose yet, Angel Raffaella."

"Then you'll have to give up the next one you get," said Raffaella crossly. "Now give me your card please, Ella."

Ella reluctantly did as she was told.

Raffaella touched her wand to Ella's card. There was a flash and then once more the card was just a dull white-gray color.

"My halo has faded as well," gasped Ella, looking around her and realizing she didn't have quite the same glittery glow surrounding her as she had since she got the stamp.

"It has indeed," Raffaella said. "Now, back to school. You will both go to the Sad Cloud tomorrow as a punishment. I'm very disappointed."

As she turned to go, Ella turned to her friends. She was trying not to cry.

"Oh, Ella," said Jess, giving her a hug. "You must have known Primrose was trying to get you to do something bad so your stamp would be taken away."

Ella swallowed. "I know. I just lost my temper. Oh, I'm a useless angel!"

"No you're not. You'll get another stamp in no time at all," Tilly told her.

A terrible thought struck Ella. "But what if I don't? What if that was my one chance this week and now I've messed up?" She looked at her friends in horror. "What if I don't get to go to the start-of-term garden party after all?"

CHAPTER 7

A Special Idea

THE NEXT DAY, ELLA HAD TO SPEND THE whole of the morning between breakfast and break in the Sad Cloud with Primrose. The Sad Cloud was a dark cloud floating above the hall with a round room inside it. Everything was dull and gray and there was nothing to do when you were in there but read old books on angel history and the angel rules. Ella had spent the whole time ignoring Primrose and reading a book called *Famous Angels Past and Present,*

while Primrose had spent her time reading out the angel rules from the handbook and smirking. Ella had got back to the dorm just before the others, who had all been at a forgetting spell class.

Jess and Poppy came to find her. "Hi," Jess said giving her a sympathetic look. "Was the Sad Cloud horrible?"

"*Really* horrible," sighed Ella. "Just imagine being cooped up with Primrose for all that time!"

The other two shuddered at the thought.

"So how was the class?" Ella went on.

"Great," said Poppy. "We were learning how to help people to forget sadness."

"We got to use our wands and angel magic," said Jess. "But because we're such young angels the spells wear off pretty quickly—although Poppy was really good at them."

"You too. We got a halo stamp each," Poppy said. She went red. "Oh! We weren't going to tell you that yet."

"Don't be silly!" Ella pushed down the stab of jealousy and jumped up and hugged her friends. "I'm really happy for you."

"Really?" said Jess. "We thought you would mind."

"Of course not." The last thing Ella wanted was her friends to feel bad about getting halo stamps. "I really *am* happy. Did Tilly get one too?"

"Well, Tilly wasn't there," said Jess.

"We thought she must be sick and be up here," said Poppy. "She was really quiet at breakfast."

Ella nodded. She'd noticed that Tilly had been very quiet too. "I wonder where she can be. Should we go and look for her?"

Poppy looked torn. "We've got to go and get our stamps. We were told to go see the Archangel at break time."

"But then we really should look for Tilly," said Jess anxiously.

"Look, you go and get your stamps, I'll go and look for Tilly," said Ella.

And, jumping down off her cloud, she headed off down the hallway.

But Tilly wasn't in any of the other dorms. So Ella went down the spiral staircase to the floor below. Some angels were doing their homework in the classrooms, but there was no sign of Tilly. Where was she? Now that she thought about it, Ella realized Tilly had been quiet the evening before, too.

She checked the halls and then went outside, walking around the outside of the building, calling Tilly's name. She had almost given up hope of finding her when Ella suddenly caught sight of Tilly in the school vegetable patch with a rake in her hand.

"Tilly!" Ella said in relief. "What are you doing out here? Everyone's been worried about you. . . ." She broke off as she realized that Tilly had been crying. "What's the matter?" she asked.

Tilly sniffed, wiping a muddy hand across her face. "I'm not feeling great."

"But if you're sick you should be inside. You'll get into trouble and—"

"I'm not sick and it's okay, Seraphina knows I'm here. She said I could come out." Tilly swallowed. "I've been feeling really homesick, Ella. I miss my mom and my dad, and my brothers and sisters, too. I couldn't sleep much last night and so I went to see Seraphina after breakfast. She told me I could

miss the forgetting class and come out here instead. It reminds me of home, you see. I used to help Mom with the garden."

Ella put an arm around her. "You poor thing. But you'll see your family on holidays." She wished there was something she could do. Tilly looked so sad. "Cheer up. Just think about all the fun things we're learning—and there's the garden party on Saturday to look forward to as well. That's only three days away. We should be concentrating on getting halo stamps so we can go to that! Poppy and Jess both got halo stamps in forgetting class today."

Tilly looked rather sheepish. "Actually, I got one this morning too. For helping Seraphina weed the garden."

"Oh, Tilly!" Ella gave her friend a big hug. "That's great." Inside she could feel a fluttering of panic. *All* her friends had halo stamps now. That meant they could go to the party. Surely, surely she wasn't going to be the only one left behind. She didn't think she could bear it if that happened!

"Thanks for coming to find me," said Tilly.

"I'll just go and put this rake away and then I'll come back inside."

"Okay," said Ella. "Don't be long. We'll have forgotten what you look like!"

"I won't." Tilly forced a smile.

Ella headed back into the building to tell Poppy and Jess that she had found Tilly. She wished she could think of something to cheer Tilly up. But what?

Ella thought about it. Tilly loved gardening. And what did gardens have in them—not just vegetables, but flowers. Flowers. That was it! And not just any old flower! An idea started to form in Ella's mind. What was it that Raffaella had said earlier about the remembering flower—about how it made people feel happy? Raffaella hadn't said how it worked, but it sounded amazing.

I could get one for Tilly, Ella thought. But then she paused. The flower was at Rainbow's End, and that was out of bounds. It would stop her from going to the party altogether if she was caught. But it would be such an adventure and it would help Tilly. . . .

Ella felt a leap of excitement. She'd do it! She just needed to get into Archangel Grace's office and copy the directions down. She could go tomorrow morning when everyone went to assembly.

Ella gave a little skip. She was going to have an adventure. She couldn't wait!

CHAPTER 8

Rainbow's End

F OR THE REST OF THAT DAY, ELLA TRIED to make sure Tilly was never alone so she didn't feel homesick. When Seraphina announced there was going to be a quiz competition after supper, Tilly excused herself to go up to the dorm and Ella went with her.

"You don't have to come," said Tilly.

"I want to," said Ella. "What should we do?"

They settled on drawing. Ella loved drawing, and Tilly had a book from home with pictures of the most magical places from around Angel World. She liked tracing the pictures and then coloring them in.

"That's really good," said Tilly, as Ella finished a drawing of the Angel Academy. She inspected it. "Glittery! Look, there's Seraphina and Archangel Grace, and you've even drawn the butterflies and dragonflies outside. I wish I could draw like you."

"It's a pity drawing isn't a real angel talent," said Ella.

"I've read somewhere that drawing is an important angel skill," said Tilly.

"It can't be," Ella pointed out. "If it was that important we'd have drawing classes, and we don't."

"I guess," Tilly agreed. "I do like your picture though."

Ella smiled. "Here. You can have it." She handed it over.

"Thank you!" Tilly tacked it up to the wall by her bed. "I love it!"

Ella was glad that she had made Tilly happy. *She'll be even happier soon,* she thought. Hugging her secret close, Ella smiled to herself as she thought about her plan.

The next morning when the bell rang for assembly, Ella hung back. "You go ahead. I'll be down in a minute," she told her friends.

Instead of heading for the hall, Ella headed for Archangel Grace's office. She lingered beside a large marble statue of another famous archangel in the hallway, pretending to examine it with great interest, while she waited for the hallway to clear of people. Once she was alone, she hurried to the door. Thinking she heard footsteps behind her, she glanced around, but the hallway was empty. It must have been just her imagination.

Heart pounding, Ella knocked on the door. When there was no answer, she turned the handle. The room was empty and the book was on the desk. Ella shut the door behind her and ran over. She started flicking through the pages, trying to stifle the different sounds that came out as she looked through it. Finally she found it—Rainbow's End. And here—she traced a line with her fingers—was the Guardian Angel Academy.

She frowned, looking from one place to the other. It didn't look so far.

Quickly she pulled a little notebook out of her pocket and started to sketch—north to Bluebell Woods via Honeysuckle Way, then west to Craggy Peaks. That part looked quite complicated, but from there she should be able to see the rainbow. Once she reached it all she had to do was land on it, slide down it, and that was that!

Quickly Ella gave it a last once-over—just to check she had it right. Then she put the pad back in her pocket and crept over to the door. Left . . . Right . . . The coast was clear.

She smiled. "Rainbow's End here I come," she said.

Behind the statue, an angel with big blue eyes hid and watched her. . . .

Ella couldn't wait to get going, but one look at the weather outside, as she made her way down to the assembly hall, told her that she would have to wait. The rain was lashing down hard and the clouds were dark and gloomy.

The next day was just the same. And the one after. It wasn't until Saturday that the weather improved. As Ella pushed back the curtains and sunlight flooded the dorm, excitement flooded through her. Today was the day!

The only blot on her happiness was the thought of the party later on. She still hadn't managed to get another halo stamp, and if she didn't get one she wouldn't be going to the party. *I'll have to try to do lots of good things when I get back,* she thought.

Hanging behind the others as they headed for their sewing silver linings class, she slipped into the gardens. This was it! Her adventure was about to begin!

In no time at all, she was off. She flew into the air and rose high above the woods, and then swooped across to Honeysuckle Way, breathing in the sweet scent from below. After Honeysuckle Way, it was on to the mountains. It was harder then, the wind blew her this way and that and her route twisted and turned. "Come on! Keep going!" she muttered to herself. She beat her wings as fast as she could until finally she saw what she was looking for—a perfect rainbow stretched across the sky!

With a final burst of speed, she flew straight to the top of its arch. As she reached it, she was enveloped in a glow of magical colors. She spun around and around for a few seconds before managing to sit down. "Wow!" she gasped as she started to slide downward. She went faster and faster, her hair streaming out behind her. A few seconds later, she burst out in a shower of multicolored sparkles at the end.

She gasped as she bumped onto the soft grass. Rainbow's End! She was here! Jumping to her feet, she saw that it really was the most magical place. Dragonflies flew from flower to flower and fireflies buzzed in the air. Ella looked all around her at the haze of purple flowers carpeting the grass. There were remembering flowers everywhere! She bent down to pick one up and held it in her hands. She waited for a moment to see if she felt suddenly happy. When she didn't, she turned it around in her hands, lifting up the petals and touching the center. A riot of sparkles exploded, cascading up around her like a fireworks show.

"Oh, halos and wings!" Ella breathed. "Tilly will love it!"

There wasn't time to hang around. Turning from the sparkles, she got out the map. Now to check her way home.

The flower in one hand, map in the other, Ella spread it out. She was very glad she had it. The journey had been so twisty and turny, getting home without it would be impossible. All the mountains looked the same. But as she pushed it down, the paper flew up as a gust of wind blew across the clearing.

"Oh, just stay still for one minute, will you?" she said in exasperation.

Then, just as she was trying to look at the paper, there was an extra-heavy gust of wind and it blew out of her hand! Ella went to catch it but, just as she did, another gust blew it even farther away. Every time she neared it, it blew on until, with one last gust of wind, it flew right over the edge of the ravine.

"No!" Ella gasped, but it was no use. The map was gone—and without it she would never find her way back to school!

CHAPTER 9

Missing!

"WHERE CAN SHE HAVE GONE?" POPPY said to Jess and Tilly after their sewing silver linings class.

"I don't know," said Jess, "but I hope she turns up soon."

"Looking for your friend by any chance?" a voice asked behind them.

Tilly sighed. "Come to stir up trouble, Primrose?"

"Trouble? Me?" Primrose looked all inno-

cence. "Of course not. I just thought maybe you'd like to know where Ella is."

"Do you know where she is?" Poppy demanded.

"Oh yes. She's gone to Rainbow's End!"

The other three angels stared at her.

"Don't be stupid!" Tilly said. "Ella hasn't gone to Rainbow's End. It's out of bounds."

Primrose tossed her head. "Well, all I can say

is I saw her coming out of Archangel Grace's office three days ago talking about Rainbow's End and holding something that looked like a map. Now she's gone missing. Who's the stupid one now?" She smiled primly. "Archangel Grace had really better be told about it. After all, third-grade angels must never go out of bounds."

She tossed her ringlets and walked away.

Tilly looked at the others in dismay. "If Primrose is telling the truth, Ella's going to be in real trouble!"

"Ella wouldn't go to Rainbow's End!" Jess said.

Poppy groaned. "Well, she does like adventure—she tried to get me to go exploring with her on our very first day, but Primrose stopped us. . . ."

"Well, this time we've got to stop Primrose telling the Archangel!" Tilly said.

Poppy gasped. "I know how! . . . Primrose!" she shouted.

Primrose turned. "Yes?"

Pulling out her wand, Poppy ran toward her. "Higgle piggle, place a bet, make this angel truly forget."

"What the—" Primrose's mouth opened and shut as a sparkle of glitter cascaded over

her. She blinked a few times. "Where am I?" she said dazedly.

"At angel school," said Poppy.

"Oh." Primrose gave her a curious look. "Who are you? Are you my friend?"

"Well . . . um . . ."

Primrose looked Poppy up and down. "You're not very tidy, are you? But I suppose if we're friends, we're friends!" She linked arms with Poppy. "Hello, friend."

Poppy sent a help-what-do-I-do-now? look to Jess and Tilly.

"Are you my friends too?" Primrose asked them happily.

"Yes . . . um, I suppose we're your friends," said Tilly, coming forward.

"You know, I'm sure I was about to go and do something, but I can't seem to remember what it was," said Primrose, frowning.

"It can't have been anything very important," Jess said quickly.

"Definitely not," agreed Poppy and Tilly.

"You're probably right," agreed Primrose.

Just then, Seraphina walked around the corner. "Girls, what are you doing here? You're going to be late for your gardening class."

"Who are you?" Primrose asked.

Seraphina frowned. "What do you mean, Primrose?"

"Primrose? Who's Primrose?" said Primrose, looking startled.

"You are, of course," said Seraphina.

"I'm not Primrose," said Primrose.

"Is this some sort of a joke?" said Seraphina.

"A joke," said Primrose indignantly. "No."

"We'll just be getting along to class," Poppy said hastily.

And with Seraphina watching them in astonishment, the three friends grabbed Primrose and hurried her away.

CHAPTER 10

To the Rescue!

THANKFULLY THE NEXT CLASS WAS angel gardening and it was reasonably easy to hide at the bottom of the garden with Primrose, keeping out of the teacher's way. Primrose seemed happy to believe she was their friend, although Veronica kept giving her astounded looks from the other side of the flower beds.

"We're going to have to do something," Tilly whispered urgently to Jess and Poppy,

while Primrose was busy learning how to use magic to persuade sunflower seeds to grow into flowers. "We might have stopped Primrose telling Archangel Grace for the moment, but the magic will wear off soon and Ella's still missing. We're just lucky that the teachers haven't noticed yet, but it won't be long. . . ."

Jess looked worried. "Surely she shouldn't

be gone this long, even if she has gone to Rainbow's End."

"Unless . . ." Tilly swallowed. "Unless something has happened and she's in trouble?"

Jess bit her lip. "What are we going to do?"

"There's only one thing," said Poppy. "We'll have to go after her."

"But we don't know the way and we haven't got a map," Jess pointed out.

"I suppose we could always sneak into Archangel Grace's study," said Poppy, uncertainly.

They all looked at one another. Even though they wanted to find Ella, none of them liked the idea at all.

"I know!" gasped Tilly suddenly. "My book! The one I brought from home. It's got pictures of all the most magical places in Angel World. It has a map in the front showing where they all are. It's bound to show where Rainbow's End is!"

"Great!" said Poppy. "It's a plan, then! As soon as gardening is finished, let's go!"

At the end of the lesson, the three friends took Primrose into the library and sat her down with a thick book called *A History of the Guardian Angel Academy*. Poppy told her she had to read it all for homework.

"It should keep her busy for a while anyway," said Poppy as they hurried into the garden. "Now, have you got your book, Tilly?"

Tilly nodded.

She'd whizzed back to the dorm while the other two had been in the library. "Here!" She showed them both the map. "It looks like we've got to fly over the woods and get to Honeysuckle Way first of all, then head to Craggy Peaks. Come on!"

The three angels stood side by side and concentrated. Tilly was the first to rise off the ground, then Jess, and finally Poppy shot up like a rocket.

Taking turns to read the map and call out directions, they flew over the woods and headed north to Honeysuckle Way before twisting and turning over the peaks of the mountains. At last the rainbow came in sight.

"Now what?" gasped Jess.

"We fly into it!" said Tilly.

They grabbed one another's hands and plunged into the top. A second later, they were all whizzing down, squealing in delight.

Bump ... bump ... bump ... One by one they landed at Rainbow's End in a flurry of wings.

"Poppy, Jess, Tilly!" Jumping to their feet, they saw Ella standing, staring at them in astonishment. "What are you three doing here?"

"What do you mean, what are we doing here?" said Poppy. "We're here because of you, of course! Primrose told us where you had gone."

"When you didn't come back, we thought you must be in trouble," said Tilly. "So we came after you." She looked around. "Oh, how glittery! Isn't this an amazing place?"

"Yes, it is, but hang on." Ella was reeling

from what Poppy had said. "Did you just say Primrose knows I came here?"

"Yes, she saw you coming out of Archangel Grace's office," said Jess. "We have to get back!"

"Oh no!" Ella groaned. Her relief at seeing the others was drowned by dismay. Primrose was bound to tell the teachers. She was going to be in so much trouble. *And not just me,* she thought, looking at her friends. *All of us!*

"Are you okay?" said Poppy. "Why didn't you come back to school?"

"I lost my map," Ella said. "It flew away and I couldn't figure out how to get home."

"Don't worry," said Poppy. "We've got a map with us. But we must get back as quickly as possible."

"Poppy put a forgetting spell on Primrose," explained Tilly. "It was so funny, Ella. When Seraphina came along, Primrose couldn't even remember her own name!"

Ella giggled, the seriousness of the situation forgotten for a minute. "Really? Oh I wish I'd seen that!"

"We left her in the library, but the spell might wear off at any time," Poppy said. She grabbed Ella's hand. "Let's go!"

Using the map, they managed to get safely home. One by one, they landed in the gardens, Poppy hitting the ground with a resounding *thud*!

They ran to the library. But Primrose had disappeared!

"Oh no! What if her memory's come back?" said Tilly in alarm.

Ella felt sick. If Primrose had gone to tell Archangel Grace, they would all be in so much trouble. Maybe they would even be expelled!

They hurried back to their dorm. Just as they went inside, there was a commotion from farther along the hallway. "Get off me!"

It was Primrose's high-pitched voice. They poked their heads out.

Primrose was being helped back to her own dorm by two older angels.

"It's all right. You'll feel better after a little rest," one of them was saying soothingly.

"I don't need a rest! I have to keep doing my homework. I have to read the *whole* book!"

"No you don't," said the older angel. "You've been feeling a bit strange."

"Don't be ridiculous," said Primrose indignantly. "I'm not feeling strange at all. I'm absolutely fine!"

"Absolutely fine?" The other angel shook her head. "You couldn't even remember your own name."

"Of course I know my own name," said Primrose. "I'm ... I'm ..." She stopped and her voice took on a different tone as she started to frown. "I am Primrose de-broe Ferguson of Watersplash Lane!"

"The spell's wearing off!" Poppy hissed.

"Get your hands off me immediately," Primrose said. "I need to see Archangel Grace!"

Jess caught her breath as Primrose pulled free. "Now what?"

"We've got to stop her!" said Tilly.

"No, wait!" Ella grabbed their arms. "Let her go to Archangel Grace." She grinned at their astonished faces. "I think this could be fun!"

Five minutes later Primrose was outside their door with Archangel Grace. Her voice was full of self-importance.

"Yes, Archangel Grace. I know it's a terrible thing for an angel to do but, like I said, Ella has gone out of bounds. She's flown to Rainbow's End." They could almost hear Primrose shaking her head. "I simply don't understand how she could behave so badly. Of course, I myself would *never* go out of the school grounds. But then Ella never behaves as a proper angel should."

There was the low murmur of the Archangel's

voice and then the door was pushed open.

"See, Archangel," Primrose said, "she's not here. . . . Oh!"

Jess, Poppy, Tilly, and Ella were sitting on their beds, like perfect picture-book angels, polishing their halos.

"But . . . but . . . ," Primrose spluttered.

"Hello, Archangel Grace. Hello, Primrose," said Ella innocently. "Can we help you? We were just taking some time to polish our halos."

"And very beautiful they are looking too," Archangel Grace said, before turning and sighing. "Primrose, I really do not appreciate having my time wasted."

"But you can't be here!" Primrose spluttered to Ella. "She went to Rainbow's End!" Primrose turned to the Archangel. "She *did*!"

Archangel Grace shook her head sadly. "You're clearly not feeling very well, Primrose dear. I think you'd better spend the rest of the day quietly in bed."

"But it's the party!" gasped Primrose. "And I've got a halo stamp."

"I really don't think it would be wise for you to attend. Come on now, dear. Back to bed. I'll ask one of the older angels to bring you up a dinner tray later."

Primrose took one last look at Ella, Poppy, Jess, and Tilly—who were giving her sympathetic looks. *"Gahhhh!"* she cried, and she flounced out of the door.

Archangel Grace sighed and shook her head. "Poor Primrose. She seems very out of sorts today. I'm sorry to have disturbed you, girls."

She turned to go, when something caught her eye.

"What a beautiful picture." She pointed to the painting on the wall next to Tilly's bed. She turned to Tilly. "Is it yours?"

"It is now," said Tilly. "But I didn't draw it. Ella did."

"It's beautiful," said Archangel Grace. "Such a good picture of the school." She smiled. "And there I am too. It would look wonderful on my study wall."

"You can have it!" Tilly said, quickly. She turned to Ella. "See, I told you so. Drawing *is* a skill."

"A very highly valued angel skill indeed," said Archangel Grace. "Why? Did you think it wasn't, Ella?"

"Well, yes," Ella admitted. "We don't have drawing classes, do we? They're not mentioned in the handbook."

"That's because your handbook is for third-grade angels in their first term. You will certainly be doing drawing classes next term and I am sure Angel Gabriella, our art teacher, will be delighted to know she has such a talented student to teach. Well done on such a lovely picture, Ella. You really must have a halo stamp for it. Come to my study and collect it."

And with that, she turned on her heel and closed the door. The four friends looked at one another for a moment and then collapsed into giggles.

"See!" said Tilly. "Didn't I tell you drawing was a talent?"

"And I thought I only had a talent for getting into trouble!" Ella said.

Poppy hugged her. "Now that you've got your halo stamp, you can come to the party!"

"While poor Primrose has to stay in bed with a dinner tray," said Tilly. They all giggled again.

"I'm just glad we got back from Rainbow's

End without being discovered!" said Jess in relief.

"Why *did* you go there, Ella?" said Tilly.

Ella remembered, and reaching into her pocket, she pulled out the purple flower. It was rather crumpled, but still in one piece. "I went to get this for Tilly. It's a remembering flower. Do you remember Raffaella told us that they can make people happy? I hoped that if Tilly held it, it might make her less homesick." She held it out.

Tilly caught her breath. "Oh, Ella. That's so nice of you."

"Try it," Ella urged. "You have to touch the center."

Tilly took the flower and touched the center. A fountain of silver sparkles cascaded out, just like they had back at Rainbow's End. "It's totally glittery, isn't it?" said Ella happily, as the sparkles filled the air and her three friends squealed. "I mean, anyone's going to feel happier if they're surrounded by sparkles, aren't they?"

"Wait!" said Jess suddenly. "I don't think it's just the sparkles that make the person holding the flower happier. Look!"

Ella stared. In the center of the sparkles a picture was forming. It showed four angels, a man, a woman, and two little girls.

"Oh my goodness! It's Mom and Dad and my sisters!" cried Tilly. "Oh wow!" Her face split into a grin as she looked at them.

"It didn't work like that for me," said Ella, puzzled.

"The flower must work for people who

really need it—by showing you people who make you happy!" realized Jess.

"It's wonderful!" said Tilly. "I love it!"

As she spoke the picture changed and became a picture of Ella, Poppy, and Jess all laughing, just as they had been a few moments ago.

"Now it's showing you us!" said Ella in surprise. "That's odd."

Tilly's eyes shone. "No it's not. It's because you all make me happy too!"

Ella, Poppy, and Jess hugged her. After a few moments the sparkles faded. Tilly sighed happily. "Thank you for my flower, Ella."

"Do you feel a bit less homesick now?" Ella asked hopefully.

Tilly nodded. "I really do. Today's been so much fun." She smiled around at them all.

"You know, I think I'm actually just as happy at school as I am at home."

"Good. Angel school is fantastic!" said Ella.

"And do you know something else that's going to be fantastic?" said Poppy.

They all grinned. "The party!" they chorused.

The party *was* fantastic. It was held in Archangel Grace's special private garden. Giant butterflies the size of dinner plates fluttered in the air, and bright flowers filled the marble pots and tubs. Seraphina was conjuring up sticks of pink cotton candy and Angel Celestine was making lollipops grow on the golden trees. Some of the teachers were playing music so people could dance, and at the end of the garden, there was a massive rainbow slide. It

wasn't quite as amazing as sliding down the real rainbow, but it was loads of fun!

"*Whee!*" cried Ella as she whizzed down it.

"*Whee!*" yelled Poppy crashing into her.

They pulled each other to their feet, laughing, and looked to where Jess and Tilly were swinging each other around to the music. "Hasn't today been great?" said Ella happily.

"Oh yes!" said Poppy. "Our first real adventure. I hope we have lots more!"

"We will," Ella promised. "We really will!" Her eyes sparkled as she looked around the garden. She had a feeling that the fun had only just begun!

Birthday Surprise

For Tula Knowles,
a perfect angel

The Guardian Angel Academy Third-Grade Fireworks Show

CHAPTER 1

An Important Announcement

W HAT'S GOING ON?" ELLA BROWN fluttered down the spiral staircase at the Guardian Angel Academy, coming to land at the bottom next to her friend, Tilly. The hallway was crammed full of angels gathered around a sign, and excited chatter filled the air. *Something* was definitely happening!

"Come and look at this!" Tilly pulled Ella through the crowd. "Excuse me! Excuse me, please," she said to the other angels until they reached the front.

The sign was glittery and sparkly and kept changing color. "*The Guardian Angel Academy Third-Grade Fireworks Show*," Ella read aloud. "*Friday the twenty-fifth of October.* Oh, angel-tastic!" she exclaimed, pushing her dark brown hair behind her ears. "We're having a fireworks show in three days."

"I know!" said Tilly, her eyes shining. "It's the day our parents come to take us home for the midterm break."

Ella clutched her arm. "Look—the paper's changing again!" They watched excitedly as the paper turned purple.

Tilly read the words. "*All third-grade angels will be expected to take part in the show.*"

Ella caught her breath. "So we're all going to actually *perform* in the fireworks show?"

"Yes, indeed," came a voice from behind them. Everyone swung around. Angel Seraphina, Ella and Tilly's class tutor, was standing there. "Every third-grade angel will get a turn at carrying the different lights through the sky, and the very best angel will get a starring role in the finale."

"Oh, halos and wings!" breathed Ella.

"That would be really scary," said Tilly, her eyes wide.

"It would be amazing!" said Ella, imagining everyone watching her as she swooped and dived, setting off fireworks in the sky.

"One thing's for sure, you're all going to have fun whether you have a starring role or not." Angel Seraphina smiled. "And I'm sure your parents will enjoy watching the show, before taking you home for the midterm break. However, if you want that starring role you'd better practice your flying." Angel Seraphina flew away.

Ella turned to Tilly. "I've seen a fireworks show before, but to actually take part in one—maybe have the main part—wouldn't that be *totally glittery!*"

"I wouldn't get too excited, Ella Brown," came a haughty voice from behind them.

"It's not likely *you'll* get the starring role, is it?"

Ella turned and saw Primrose standing there. She was the most annoying angel in the whole school. With her sparkling blue eyes, and pretty blonde hair curled into ringlets, she looked perfectly angelic—but she so wasn't.

Ella felt Tilly shrink back—Tilly hated arguments—but *she* wasn't scared of Primrose. "And why shouldn't I get the starring role?" she demanded.

"Didn't you hear what Angel Seraphina said?" Primrose nudged the angel standing beside her, who had red hair and giggled when prompted. "Only the *best* angel will get the starring role. And one thing's for certain—you *definitely* don't fall into that category." Her eyes swept snootily over Ella. "All you're best at is getting into trouble!"

Ella put her hands on her hips. "You've been sent to the Sad Cloud as often as me, Primrose."

"Ella, don't get into an argument now," Tilly pleaded, tugging her arm. "You heard what Angel Seraphina said—everyone will get to take part in the show. It doesn't really matter who has the starring role."

"Come on, Veronica." Primrose turned to her friend. "We've got better things to do with our time than stand around talking to troublemakers like Ella." And with that she flounced off.

"Right! That's it!" Ella sprang after her.

Tilly grabbed her. "No, Ella! Ignore her.

She's just trying to make you mad so you get into trouble."

Ella stopped herself. Tilly was right. Primrose loved to make her lose her temper—usually when there was a teacher around. Angels were *never* supposed to lose their temper. It said so in the handbook that all the third-grade angels had been given a copy of. "All right, I won't go after her," said Ella, "but she is just so annoying! I hope she doesn't get the starring role in this show." *And I hope I do,* she added to herself.

"Forget Primrose," said Tilly. "Let's find the others and tell them all about the fireworks show."

Ella and Tilly hurried outside into the courtyard, where they found Poppy and Jess, their other two best friends, sitting underneath the marble statue of their founder, Archangel Emmanuel. Jess was bouncing a ball back and forth against a wall and they were sharing cloudberry cookies, their white halos gleaming in the sun. Archangel Emmanuel had been sculpted in full song, mouth open, eyes wide. It was one of Ella's favorite statues in the school grounds.

"Where have you two been?" Poppy asked. As usual, her curly blonde hair looked like a bird had been nesting in it, and the rest of her looked just as messy—her white dress even had a splotch of sauce from breakfast! Jess was much neater—her dark hair was tied back in a ponytail, and her uniform was clean.

"We've been finding out something very exciting," said Ella. "Now," she pretended to tease, "shall we tell them, Tilly? Or shall we not?"

"Tell us!" said Poppy eagerly.

"Well . . . guess what *we'll* be doing in three days," said Ella.

"What?" Poppy said.

"Only performing in a fireworks show!" Ella exclaimed. She quickly explained about the sign.

"Oh, glittersome!" exclaimed Poppy.

"Just think how totally sparkly it will be to take part in a fireworks show," enthused Tilly.

Ella looked at Jess. The dark-haired angel was sitting quietly. "It's really exciting, isn't it, Jess?" Ella said, surprised her friend hadn't said anything.

"Yeah . . . yeah, sure it is," muttered Jess. Ella frowned. Jess didn't sound that excited. But then Jess was kind of shy—maybe she didn't like the idea of performing in front of everyone.

Before Ella could ask her if that was what it was, the school bell rang. "Time to go," said Tilly, pulling Poppy up. "We don't want to be late for class."

A bluebird who had been circling around the head of the statue swooped down and pecked up the crumbs from their cloudberry cookies. His coat shone in different shades of indigo and turquoise and his dark eyes sparkled like jewels.

"Look at him. Isn't he beautiful!" said Tilly.

"Bluebirds are supposed to be lucky," commented Ella.

"He'll be very *unlucky* for us if looking at him makes us late for Angel Gabriella's class!" said Tilly, setting off. "Come on, all of you! I don't want to lose any halo stamps today."

Halo stamps were what you earned for good behavior, and all of the angels at the Academy had halo cards for them. This being their first year, the third graders had been told that when they filled up their card, the color of their halo and uniform would change, and their wings would grow a bit bigger. All the third graders still had the white halos and white dresses they had started with at the beginning of term a few weeks ago, but the next level up was a sparkling sapphire-blue, and they all wanted to change to that. But they had to be careful—halo stamps could also be taken away for lateness, untidiness, and generally behaving in ways that angels shouldn't.

"How many halo stamps have you all got now?" Poppy asked.

"Four," said Tilly.

"Four! That's fabulous," said Poppy. "I've got three."

"Well, I've only got two," sighed Ella.

"You would have had three if you hadn't had one taken away for that flying tangle with Primrose last month," Tilly pointed out.

"True," Ella said. "What about you, Jess? Jess . . . ?" Ella looked around. Jess was still standing at the foot of the statue, lost in thought. "Jess, come on!" Ella went back for her. "What are you doing? You should be coming to class with us."

"Oh, sorry," Jess said distractedly. "I was just thinking about something."

"Is it the fireworks show?" Ella asked. "Are you worried about performing?"

Jess looked surprised. "Oh no, I'm not worried about that. I wouldn't want a main part anyway. It'll be nice just being in the background."

"Oh. So what's the matter?" Ella said.

"I'm fine. Nothing's the matter. Nothing at all." Jess quickly flew after the others.

Ella frowned as she watched her go. Jess could say what she liked, but she was beginning to feel sure something was up with her friend. What could it possibly be?

CHAPTER 2

Heavenly Animals

THE FOUR ANGELS FLUTTERED ACROSS the courtyard and flew into the hallway on the opposite side. It was a tall room, covered from wall to ceiling with iridescent moons and stars. Two chandeliers dangled from the ceiling, sparkling like diamonds, and making it look like the most magical starry night ever.

"Come on," said Tilly, speeding up. All of the third-grade angels' flying had improved loads since they had started at the school a few

weeks ago. "You all go on ahead," called Jess. "I want to check the mail room first."

"Why?" said Ella, stopping, her wings fluttering.

The mail pigeons only delivered once a day and the four of them had already checked the pigeonholes that morning.

Jess shrugged. "I just do."

"I'll come with you, then," Ella offered. Leaving Tilly and Poppy to fly on, she followed Jess into the mail room. There was a row of pigeonholes made out of shining gold. Each student had their own pigeonhole with their name written underneath it in sparkling sapphires. By the window, the mail pigeons perched on jeweled stands. The pigeons had their heads tucked under their golden wings, resting before they set off to get more mail that evening. There were a few older angels also checking their pigeonholes. Jess checked hers. As Ella had suspected, it was still empty.

"Are you expecting something, Jess?" one of the older angels asked.

"Yes," sighed Jess.

"Me too." The angel shrugged. "I've been waiting for days. There are quite a few of us who seem to be missing packages. Isn't it strange?"

Jess nodded. "I was sure there would be something here. . . ."

"What are you expecting?" Ella asked her curiously.

"It's not important," said Jess, swallowing hard and flying out of the room.

Ella flew after her. "But—"

"I don't want to talk about it, Ella!" Jess said sharply.

Ella blinked. Jess never snapped. What was the matter with her? She wanted to ask more but she didn't want to upset Jess, so she decided to keep quiet. They flew to the second floor where the maze of hallways divided off, leading to different classrooms. As they neared the room where their heavenly animals class was taking place, a loud, unmistakable voice floated out. Primrose!

"Another halo stamp for neatness," she was saying smugly. "I've got seven now. It's only to be expected, of course! I am always so neat and tidy."

"Not always very modest though," Ella muttered under her breath. They flew in to find Primrose showing everyone the holographic stamp that Angel Gabriella had just awarded her.

"All right, angels, settle down," said Angel Gabriella. "Ella . . . Jess . . . you got here just in time. Take your places quickly, please, and let's get started." Angel Gabriella always reminded Ella of a bun—she was very round and had black eyes just like little currants. They were usually kind and twinkly, but she didn't tolerate any nonsense.

"Over here, Ella," called Tilly, indicating the spaces that

she and Poppy had saved for them at a table. There were pads of paper and paint out for all the angels. Ella felt excited. They didn't usually do art in their heavenly animals class, but she loved drawing and painting.

"This looks fun! What does Angel Gabriella want us to do today?" whispered Ella, grabbing a jar of glittery paint, a brush, and some water before sitting herself down in the chair beside Tilly and leaning over her paper.

"We've each got to choose a different heavenly animal to paint," Tilly whispered back. "I'm painting a phoenix. What will you do?"

"I'll try a winged horse," said Ella. Happiness sparkled through her. Lost in her painting, her hands flew over the page, flicking this way and that as she dipped her brush in and out of the dish of water. Finally, she stopped and looked up.

"Let's see," said Tilly.

Ella turned the pad around.

"Oh, Ella, it's amazing!" said Tilly.

"What's amazing?" Primrose came over.

"Look!" Tilly said, placing the pad back down on the table.

Primrose moved dangerously close to the dish of water. "Hmm, let me see."

Tilly grabbed the dish of water just before Primrose spilled it.

"Whoops, silly me," said Primrose, arching her eyebrows. "I wouldn't want to ruin your lovely painting, Ella." She reached out for the picture again, this time her elbow catching intentionally against a jar of blue paint.

"Careful!" Jess gasped, grabbing the jar before it could spill all over Ella's picture.

"Thanks, Jess," said Ella quickly.

"Oh, dearie me, I am being clumsy today," said Primrose.

"Look, Primrose, can you just go away?" Ella said through gritted teeth. She glanced over and saw Angel Gabriella look in their direction.

"But I'm only trying to look at your picture," said Primrose innocently.

"You're not," hissed Ella. "You're trying to ruin it!"

Primrose pretended to look shocked. "Me? I wouldn't do a thing like that!"

"What's going on here?" Angel Gabriella came over. "Is there a problem, angels?"

"No, no problem, Angel Gabriella." Primrose smiled sweetly. "Ella just seems to think I want to ruin her painting, but of course I'd never do anything like that. Angels must never be mean," she quoted from the school handbook. "I just wanted to admire Ella's beautiful painting."

"That's lovely of you, dear. Now, let me see, Ella," said Angel Gabriella. "Oh, it is rather good, isn't it?" Her face broke into a big, beaming smile. "I think a picture like that definitely deserves a halo stamp." With a tap from her wand, a glitter of sparkles spun out over Ella's card and the most beautiful holographic stamp appeared on it.

Ella beamed.

"Thank you for pointing Ella's picture out

to me, Primrose," said Angel Gabriella. "That was very kind of you. Now, Ella, if only you could apply yourself as well to your punctuality as you do to your drawing, you'd be the perfect angel!" She swept on to see what the rest of the class were doing. To Ella's relief, Primrose moved away, looking annoyed. She put her picture down. Then she noticed that Jess was staring glumly at her own picture.

"So how are you doing, Jess?" said Ella, going over to her. "What have you drawn?"

Jess sighed. "It's not very good."

"Let me see."

It was a bluebird like the one outside, only its legs were a little long, the beak was a little wonky, and the wings were more like the size of an eagle's.

"It's beautiful, Jess," said Ella kindly.

"You know it's not," Jess sighed. "Can you help me?"

"Well, if you change the legs a little like this"—Ella picked up her brush—"and add a little more here." She rubbed out a little on the right. . . . Finally she had finished.

"It's perfect now, Ella." Jess grinned.

"It really is. It's just like the sweet bluebird by the statue," Poppy agreed, coming around and looking at it too.

"Not all bluebirds are sweet, you know." Archangel Gabriella joined in, overhearing the conversation in passing. "They can be mischievous birds as well. Haven't you heard about the time a bluebird took Archangel Grace's brooch? They love all sorts of glittery things, and nest in the strangest places." The teacher smiled and headed off to join another group of angels.

"So what's going on here?" It was Primrose again.

"Oh, not you again, Primrose," sighed Ella.

"Well, that's not very friendly, is it?" Primrose said, looking hurt. "And there I was, coming over to see how Jess was doing as well. So what have you drawn, Jess? Oh!" Her eyes widened. "It's a blue pelican!"

Jess's face crumpled.

It was the final straw for Ella. Annoying her was one thing, but teasing one of her friends was quite another. Her temper snapped, and before she could stop herself, she had picked up the blue jar of paint and spilled it all over Primrose!

Primrose shrieked.

"Ella! What have you done?" cried Jess, covering her mouth as Poppy and Tilly both gasped in horror.

Hearing all the commotion, Angel Gabriella turned. "Angels! What *is* happening?" she cried, as Primrose stood there, blue paint dripping down her face and onto the floor.

CHAPTER 3

Missing Mail

OH NO! ELLA CRINGED AS SHE LOOKED at her furious teacher. What had she done?

"Oh, Angel Gabriella!" wailed Primrose. "Ella spilled the jar of paint on me—and look at the mess on the floor as well." She sobbed loudly and dramatically.

"Did you? Did you, Ella? Did you really do this?" demanded Angel Gabriella.

"I . . . um . . . I did," admitted Ella, her mouth feeling dry. "I'm sorry. I shouldn't have done

it, I know," she rushed on. "But Primrose was being rude about Jess's picture and—"

"That is enough!" snapped Angel Gabriella. "There can be no excuse for spilling paint on people. It is abominable behavior! That halo stamp I gave you will have to be taken back!"

"I'm very sorry, Angel Gabriella," said Ella, hanging her head. "I'll clean up the mess."

"You most certainly will," said Angel

Gabriella. "And after that, you can take yourself off to the Sad Cloud, where you can stay until you've had time to think about what you've done. I'm very disappointed in you."

Ella groaned inwardly. She hated the fact that Angel Gabriella was disappointed, and although she knew that she deserved it, she hated her punishment. The Sad Cloud was the most boring place ever—there was nothing to do there but read old books on angel history and angel rules. Still, there wasn't a thing she could do about it now. No matter how annoying Primrose had been, she shouldn't have spilled paint on her.

Angel Gabriella turned to Primrose. "Take yourself outside, Primrose, and get cleaned up. Veronica can go with you."

Sobbing as loudly as she could and glaring at

Ella, Primrose left the classroom with Veronica. Ella didn't dare to look at her friends. She got a mop and some water. Poppy, Jess, and Tilly all rushed to help her.

"No!" Angel Gabriella told them sharply. "Please leave Ella to clean up on her own. Bring your work over to this table."

Shooting Ella sympathetic looks, the other three had to do as they were told.

As she cleaned away the paint, Ella ranted at herself. How could she have done something so stupid? It was her awful temper. She was never going to be a good enough angel to be a Guardian Angel, and if she wasn't careful, all the other third-grade angels would fill their halo cards and get sapphire halos before her. She'd be the only one left with a white halo! Tears prickled in her eyes. What if Angel Gabriella decided she should be banned from the fireworks show as well? As soon as Ella had finished cleaning, she began to leave for the Sad Cloud. In the doorway she passed Primrose, coming back with Veronica.

"I'll get you back for that, Ella Brown!" hissed Primrose as she pushed past Ella, her elbows bumping Ella sharply in the ribs. "Just see if I don't."

Ella spent a very dull hour in the Sad Cloud on her own. The walls and floor were all painted gray and the seats were hard. She leafed through the books on the history of the school, but they weren't very exciting. In the end she sat down with a book and thought about her friends. She remembered how strange Jess had acted by the pigeonholes earlier. What was making her so unhappy? Ella thought about what Jess had said. She was obviously waiting for something to arrive, but what?

Ella started turning the pages of the book. The first chapter was about how the school was built. Her eyes read the words. *The school's official birthday is the first of January. . . .*

Birthday!

Of course! Ella realized something. It was Jess's birthday in two days—just before the end of term. She must have been checking the mail room to see if her parents had sent her anything yet!

Ella remembered what the older angels had

said about mail going missing. Maybe Jess's parents had sent her something and *that*, too, had gone missing.

Ella drew her knees up to her chest thoughtfully. Jess's birthday would be the first of her friends' birthdays at angel school. *We'll have to do something to celebrate,* she mused. *Especially if something is wrong with the mail and nothing arrives for Jess. We'll have to make it feel like a very special day. Tilly and Poppy and I can plan something!* Her eyes started to sparkle. *Oh yes, this is going to be fun!*

As soon as Angel Gabriella came and said Ella could leave the Sad Cloud, she set off to find her friends. It was lunchtime. As she hurried down the stairs and into the maze of hallways, she looked through each of the classroom windows—but they weren't there. They must have gone back to the dorm.

She flew up to the next floor and hurried off down the hallway that led to the turrets. As she flew, she whizzed past planets and stars covering the floors and ceilings, before coming to a halt just beside the mail room. She'd check one more time, just in case something had arrived for Jess after all.

As she started to peer around the door, something stopped her in her tracks—the sight of two people talking. It was Archangel Grace and the gardening teacher, Angel Celestine, and they were talking quite intently. The half-moon glasses on the end of Archangel Grace's nose were waggling as she spoke and her enormous gossamer wings were trembling in agitation.

"Whatever is going on, Celestine?" she was saying. "I don't understand it. Packages and letters keep disappearing. It's most puzzling."

"I know . . . ," Angel Celestine answered. "As far as I can tell, the pigeons are arriving with the mail as usual, but then before anyone gets to their pigeonholes in the morning, things disappear, and often people who have been expecting packages and letters aren't getting them. I don't understand what's happening."

Archangel Grace looked grave. "It's clear that someone must be taking them."

Angel Celestine gasped. "But who would do such a thing?"

Ella sucked in her breath. Surely no angel would steal mail? She was horrified at the thought. But Archangel Grace was right—if packages were arriving and then disappearing, someone had to be taking them.

"It simply must be one of the angels," Archangel Grace said, shaking her head. "I know it's hard to believe, but we must find the culprit."

"There you are!" A hand touched Ella's shoulder, making her nearly jump out of her skin.

"Tilly . . . Poppy . . ." Ella breathed, relieved that it was only her friends who had discovered her eavesdropping. "What are you doing here?"

"Looking for you, silly," said Tilly.

"Where's Jess?" Ella asked.

"She offered to help Angel Seraphina clean up our classroom," said Poppy.

"Fabulous!" said Ella, suddenly remembering what she had been thinking about in the Sad Cloud. "Then let's get to our dorm. I've got something I need to talk to you about and I don't want Jess to hear. . . ."

CHAPTER 4

Flying Frenzy

"JESS'S BIRTHDAY! HOW COULD WE ALL have forgotten?" Tilly and Poppy each sat on one of the little floating clouds that doubled as beds in their dorm.

"If there's a chance that Jess's mail *has* gone missing—that she's not going to get any birthday presents from her parents—then that's all the more reason to do something extra-special for her," said Poppy.

"But what?" wondered Tilly.

"Hmm." Ella frowned and looked around their dorm. It was a cozy room with a large oval window looking out over the grounds, and it had four white closets and four dressing tables, each with one of their names in large golden letters. "A party would be the obvious choice, but her birthday's Thursday and we've got fireworks show practice all day and then we're going home on Friday, so we won't have time for one."

"That's true," said Tilly.

"We need to think of something else," said Poppy.

They all racked their brains. But it wasn't so easy to think of something. What could they possibly do?

Soon, Jess joined them and the three friends had to stop talking about it. After lunch they had flying class. Now each and every one of them were able to raise themselves off the ground and fly around, but carrying lights for the fireworks show in their arms was a different matter. The third-grade angels soon found that it could really throw you off balance.

"That's it, Poppy," called out the flying teacher, Angel Raffaella. "Try to imagine your wings are like a butterfly's. Keep your arms still. Gently, easy does it."

"I'm trying," Poppy called through gritted teeth, as she managed to raise herself off the ground with a light in her hand and flutter into the sky, only to lose her balance and come crashing down again.

Ella concentrated on flying up high, and before she knew it, she was up, up, and away.

"Whoa!" she called, wobbling a bit as she clutched the light in one hand and tried to steer with the other arm.

"That's it, Ella, you're doing really well," encouraged Angel Raffaella.

Ella began to get the hang of it. She looked across the sky to see how everyone else was doing. Some of the angels were still stuck on the ground, while others were managing to raise themselves up, only to fall down again. Ella looked across and saw Primrose gliding smoothly across the sky, her ringlets flying out behind her, her light held securely in her hands. Angels and wings! Annoyingly, it looked like Primrose was rather good at flying while carrying a light. Ella bit down on her tongue as she watched Primrose pirouetting around.

"Very good, Primrose," Angel Raffaella called after a while. "You're a natural. Now, I've had a chance to watch you all, so if you could gather around, I've got an announcement to make about the show."

One by one, the angels came back down before gathering in a group in front of Angel Raffaella. The flying teacher started.

"Well," she said, "as you know, I have been asked to make a choice on who should have the starring role at the fireworks show, and on the basis of today's class, I'd like to say that I've chosen"—she paused and smiled—"Primrose de-broe Ferguson."

"That's me! It's me!" Primrose could hardly contain herself. She jumped up and down—and then she seemed to remember herself. "Thank you, Angel Raffaella," she said meekly, clasping her hands together. "It is a complete honor to be chosen. I hope I will make you proud."

Angel Raffaella smiled warmly. "Very humbly spoken. What a good angel. I am sure you *will* make me proud, my dear."

Ella raised her eyebrows at her friends. Of all the angels, it just had to be Primrose who'd been chosen! But even she had to admit that the decision had been a fair one—Primrose had been the best in the class. As Angel Raffaella turned away, Ella forced herself to do the right thing and went over to congratulate Primrose. "Well done," she said.

"Told you I'd be the star!" Primrose crowed triumphantly. "And I hope you enjoy watching me, Ella Brown—from the back row!" She swept off, smirking in delight.

CHAPTER 5

Glitter Bomb!

ON THE WAY TO GLITTER CLASS LATER that day, all Primrose could talk about was having the starring role in the show. Ella tried very hard to ignore her. There was no way she wanted to get into trouble again.

Glitter class was great fun. They all had to learn to make the glitter bombs that they were going to set off as part of the fireworks show.

"I like your bomb, Ella," said Tilly, coming over to inspect the big, colorful glitter bomb

Ella was making. Ella had sculpted the outside from papier-mâché, and was now filling it with sparkles and streamers—all the things she wanted to explode out of it into the sky.

"Are you ready for the special ingredient, Ella?" Angel Gabriella came over and pulled out a little bottle from her pocket, before sprinkling a little dust inside the glitter bomb. "Not too much," she said, a twinkle in her eye. "We don't want too much of an explosion."

"So what's in it, Angel Gabriella?" asked Tilly curiously.

Angel Gabriella tapped the side of her nose. "Now, that's a magic secret," she smiled. "Suffice to say, there's a whole lot of angel dust as part of the mix. Third graders just need to be able to make glitter bombs and not learn how to make them explode. Now, come on everyone, show me your bombs so I can add the magic to them, too."

Angel Gabriella went around the rest of the class, tapping her little bottle into each of the glitter bombs before she finally placed the bottle back in a glass cabinet. Ella watched her closely before putting the lid on her glitter bomb, sealing it, and then covering it all over in red glitter and red hearts.

"That looks lovely, Ella," said Angel Gabriella, coming over.

"How do we make the glitter bombs go off?" Ella asked.

"Ah, more magic!" said Angel Gabriella. "Now, all of you put the lids on your glitter bombs and make a circle three times on the lids with your wands, saying:

"Glitter bomb, listen to me
You will explode, on the count of three."

The angels all did as she said.

"Now, when it's time for the fireworks show and we want the glitter bombs to go off," Angel

Gabriella went on, "all you need to do is circle your wand three times in the air and count out loud to three. Each of you will make your own glitter bomb explode. We will practice it so you are all safely out of the way when the glitter bombs explode. The magic in them is powerful and you could get hurt if you were too close. Now, put your glitter bombs over there in the pile with the others, ready for Friday."

As Ella placed her bomb into the pile, a little idea started to grow in her mind. What if . . . ? What if she made a glitter bomb for Jess's birthday on Thursday? A really big one! That would be a cherub-tastic birthday surprise! She'd need to get some of Angel Gabriella's special powder. But it would only need a pinch—and it was for a good cause. It would make Jess's birthday really special.

She thought about the school handbook and recited one of the rules in her head: *Angels should always strive to make others happy.* That was what she would be doing. She grinned to herself. She couldn't wait to tell Poppy and Tilly!

As soon as class was over, Jess went to check the pigeonholes one more time. Ella was quick to grab Poppy and Tilly and pull them to one side.

"Quick—while Jess isn't here. I've got it," she said triumphantly. "I know exactly what we can do for Jess's birthday. Why don't we make a glitter bomb? The biggest and best glitter bomb ever!"

She looked eagerly at them. They both looked uncertain. "I don't know, Ella . . . ," Poppy said, looking across at Tilly.

"I'm not sure about it either," said Tilly. "I mean, we're really only just beginners. What if it goes wrong?"

"It won't go wrong!" said Ella airily. "We just make a bomb, like we have just now but bigger, and sneak a tiny pinch of Angel Gabriella's magic dust, and that's it!"

"Well, you were pretty good at making your glitter bomb," Poppy said cautiously. "Especially considering it was only our first lesson. What do you think, Tilly?"

"Maybe it'll be okay," said Tilly. "Yes, all right, I'm sure it'll be fine. I mean, it should be pretty straightforward. But not a big bomb, just a little one."

Poppy nodded. "Tilly's right. It should just be a small glitter bomb that can be contained in our dorm, so if there's any mess or anything goes wrong we can clean it up."

"But a small glitter bomb's so boring," protested Ella.

"Ella . . . ," her two friends said warningly.

"All right, all right," Ella sighed. "A small glitter bomb it is. This is going to be so much fun. I'll start designing and making it. Then all we have to do is get our hands on Angel Gabriella's special ingredient!"

The next day, they were so busy practicing for the fireworks show that Ella barely had enough time to even *think* about the glitter bomb, let alone make it! She enjoyed the practicing, though. She was almost as good as Primrose at carrying things now. As soon as Jess went off to the school Music Club after dinner, Ella, Tilly, and Poppy hurried to their dorm and started to put the birthday glitter bomb together.

"What should we put in it?" asked Tilly.

"Definitely loads of glitter," said Ella. "And some magic sparkles too. Here, let me use my wand."

"Are you sure you should?" Tilly said, anxiously.

"It'll be fine," said Ella. "I know—what about glittery letters that spell out words?" She picked up her wand and thought for a moment before waving it in the air.

"Conjure sparkly letters, a message to say:
Happy Birthday, Jess, on your special day."

"Oh, Ella, it's fabulous," cried Tilly as the letters *Happy Birthday, Jess!* appeared in large sparkly letters in the air.

"That's really clever," said Poppy, impressed. "You're so good at glitter magic, Ella!"

Feeling pleased with herself, Ella circled the letters with her wand and then tapped the glitter bomb and the letters. They popped inside the bomb, along with the other decorations, and Ella put the lid on.

"Now all we need is Angel Gabriella's special ingredient," said Poppy. "Who's going to get that?"

"I guess that should probably be me," said Ella, "seeing as it was my idea in the first place."

"Are you sure?" said Tilly, looking relieved.

"Yes, sure," said Ella. She picked up the bomb and covered it up with one of the dresses from her closet. Then, taking a look one way and then the other, Ella sneaked off down the hall with it in her arms. She was quiet as she flew, checking each of the classrooms. Most of the angels were in their dorms doing homework or at their after-school clubs.

Quickly, Ella raced down the hall, turning the corner before arriving at Angel Gabriella's room. Thankfully, the room was unlocked and she crept inside.

Tiptoeing over to the glass cabinet where she had seen Angel Gabriella put the special ingredient, she hesitated for a moment. What if it was locked? But to her relief she saw that

Angel Gabriella had left the little golden key in the lock. Gently Ella reached out and turned it. Phew! She was just about to take the bottle when she heard voices outside.

Quick as a flash, she jumped back behind the door, hugging the glitter bomb, her heart pounding. Thankfully, the footsteps passed on by. Ella waited until all was quiet and then she crept out again to the cabinet.

The red dust in the little bottle sparkled.

Ella took the bottle and pulled out the silver cork. She opened the bomb's lid and scattered a little inside—and then she stopped. How much did she need? It would be awful if it didn't go off! She put another big sprinkle into the bomb and was about to put the cork back in when she couldn't resist the temptation. She added another big sprinkle, just for luck. She knew Tilly and Poppy wanted a small glitter bomb, but where was the fun in that? She smiled to herself as she imagined Jess's stunned face as the bomb exploded. She was going to be so happy. Ella felt excitement bubble up through her. She simply couldn't wait for the next day! She loved making her friends happy.

Putting in the cork, she put the bottle back and locked the cabinet up. Then she cast the spell on the glitter bomb as Angel Gabriella had taught her and set off back to the dorm as fast as she could.

"Done it!" she cried cheerily, pushing back the door.

"That's fabulous, Ella," cried Poppy and Tilly.

"You did put only a little bit of the angel dust in though, didn't you?" Tilly asked anxiously.

"Yes, yes, just a little bit," lied Ella.

"So where shall we put it?" said Poppy, looking around the dorm.

"How about over the door," said Tilly.

"Great idea!" said Poppy. "Let's put it there now, then it will be ready for Jess tomorrow. We can set it off when we get back from assembly, before classes start. Ella, you can put a disguising spell on it so Jess won't notice."

"This is going to be just perfect!" Ella said happily, as she thought about all the angel dust inside the glitter bomb. "The best birthday surprise ever!"

CHAPTER 6

A Change of Plan

AS THE ANGELS SLEPT THAT EVENING, all was quiet, the sound of gentle breathing filling the dorm. But Ella couldn't sleep. She tossed and turned, her thoughts firmly on the glitter bomb. Surely they could do better than the door of their dorm, couldn't they? It seemed such a waste. There had to be another place for it to go off where *everyone* would see it. Then all the angels in the school would know it was Jess's birthday!

Ella's thoughts raced. Where else could she put it? Somewhere everyone would be when it went off. Suddenly an idea popped into her head. The statue of Angel Emmanuel! Everyone passed it on the way out of assembly in the morning. It was the perfect position. If she could make it explode from behind as everyone filed into the courtyard, then it would be amazing. . . .

She stopped herself. Tilly and Poppy would never agree to it. She bit her lip. Maybe . . . maybe she could put it by the statue without telling them. Okay, so they would be surprised, but they'd soon forgive her when they saw how perfect it was, wouldn't they? And when they saw Jess's face!

Yes, she'd do it. . . . Ella's mind was made up. First thing in the morning. She'd get up early, but for now it was time to get some rest. . . . And now that a plan was in place, Ella fell into a deep sleep.

When Ella woke a few hours later, the sun was just rising in the sky. The first thing she did was roll over and check the other cloud beds. They were moving gently around the room, but her friends were still quietly sleeping.

Quickly, Ella got out of bed and pulled on her clothes. Then she flew up and pulled the glitter bomb down.

All was quiet as she pushed open the door and flew along the hall, down the spiral staircase, and into the giant hallway.

She went out into the courtyard, the heavy door creaking slightly as she turned the big gold handle. The morning dew was fresh on

the ground and the rays of the early-morning sun shone down. The bluebird was circling around the statue's head again. Ella wondered where his nest was—it must be nearby.

Putting her foot onto the angel statue, she pushed herself up from the ground.

"Sorry about this, Archangel Emmanuel," she apologized to the statue as she climbed.

"I hope you don't mind me standing on you." Reaching up, she grabbed the angel's halo and used it to steady herself. Then she reached up, and carefully, very carefully, she placed the glitter bomb on the angel's shoulders before jumping back down to the ground to admire her handiwork. Last thing to do was cast a disguising spell so no one else would know it was there. She waved her wand:

*"Disguise and hide, true shape concealed,
Until it's time to be revealed."*

She smiled as the bomb faded from sight. All was ready. *If this doesn't cheer Jess up,* she thought happily, *nothing will.*

☆ ☆ ☆

It was quiet and still as Ella let herself back into the school. A troubling thought crossed her mind. What if the others had woken up and found her gone? "I know, I'll check the mail room," she said to herself. "See if there's anything there for Jess yet. I can say that's where I've been."

She ran to the pigeonholes, quickly making her way over to Jess's, and peeped inside. She let out a heavy sigh. It was still empty. It made her surer than ever that her plan was the right one. Jess had no packages to open that morning, but at least she was going to get a great, big, angel surprise!

Ella was so impatient, she could hardly eat any breakfast that morning, and she fidgeted as they went in for assembly. Jess had run down to her pigeonhole first thing but found nothing there and was looking very sad. Ella, Poppy, and Tilly had sung "Happy Birthday" to her and given her cards they had made, but although Jess had smiled, she wasn't any happier by the time they went to assembly.

Ella couldn't wait for the glitter bomb to go off. As they waited for Archangel Grace to come onto the stage and talk to them all, she nudged Jess. "Cheer up!"

Jess forced a smile. "Sorry!"

"Shhh," came a pious voice from behind them.

"Oh, do be quiet, Primrose," Ella said impatiently. "It's Jess's birthday."

But there wasn't time to get into a fight now. Archangel Grace had come onstage and begun to speak.

"Good morning, angels," she said. "This morning we will be hearing from Polly and Chloe, who will be performing the Angelic Concerto in E-flat Major." She nodded across at two angels who sat with their harps at the ready, looking nervous. "But before we do, I have a serious announcement to make. Some of you may already be aware, but it has come to my attention that over the last few days, mail seems to have been going missing from the mail room."

A low murmur ran around the room.

"Yes, indeed, you may look shocked," said Archangel Grace. "It's a worrying time for us all, and obviously someone must know what is going on. I just wanted to let you all know that I am taking it very seriously and intend to get to the bottom of it. If anyone knows anything, please come and talk to me about it."

And with that, she turned away, nodding over to the two angels with the harps, who started to play.

Ella was fizzing with excitement as the concerto came to an end and the assembly was over. She filed out with the others into the courtyard. The angels milled around, talking as they usually did. That day everyone was discussing the missing mail. Ella waited until everyone was there and then she pulled out her wand. Was this going to work? *Oh, please,* she prayed! She waved it three times, counting under her breath: "One . . . two . . . three!"

BOOM!

The glitter bomb exploded, sparkling letters forming in the air and multicolored glitter cascading down. . . . Only, it wasn't just the glitter that was flying through the air, but thick white marble dust. Ella let out a loud gasp as the glitter and dust cleared. The top half of the statue of Archangel Emmanuel had been blown to smithereens!

CHAPTER 7

Disaster!

THERE WAS A STUNNED SILENCE AS the final sprinkles of glitter and marble dust rained down. The words *Jappy Hirth Bessday* shone out in the air. Ella stood rooted to the spot. She hadn't even gotten that right....

"What the . . . ?" Archangel Grace ran forward, her bun bobbing on the back of her head as she bent toward the wreckage. "A glitter bomb!" she cried. "And behind the statue of Archangel Emmanuel. Who could have put

that there? What sort of angel would deliberately try to destroy the ancient statue of our most noble founder with a glitter bomb?"

Angel Gabriella joined her. "I'm sure there must be a reasonable explanation for this."

"A reasonable explanation?" Archangel Grace, who usually looked serene and calm, was furious. "Enough is enough. First the mail. Now this. Who is responsible for all these things? Take responsibility right now!"

Ella wanted the ground to open and swallow her up. Everyone in the school was looking around. She wanted to speak up, but how could she? Her cheeks went bright red. She opened her mouth, but Poppy clapped a hand over it to silence her.

Ella gulped. If she admitted she was to blame, the others might get into trouble too. She knew they would try and take responsibility as well, even though it had been her idea to put the bomb by the statue—and add the extra powder. Oh, why hadn't she listened to them?

"Well, has no one got anything to say?" Archangel Grace demanded.

Ella felt herself hot and itchy under the collar. The other angels murmured around her.

"The angel responsible for this must come forward," insisted Archangel Grace. "If she doesn't, then the fireworks show tomorrow will be canceled!"

"Canceled?" all the angels gasped.

Archangel Grace nodded grimly. "And when the angel in question is found—and she *will* be found, have no doubt about it—I'll expel her from the school forever!"

A little gasp went around the crowd. Ella looked across at her friends in horror. Expelled!

"Now back to your dorms," snapped Archangel Grace. "I hope by lunchtime the culprit will have come forward, and I shall be able to inform you that the show will take place as we had planned."

Ella hurried back to the dorm with the

others. Poppy and Tilly looked as shocked and pale as she did. Neither of them seemed to know what to say.

"Isn't it awful?" gasped Jess, as they shut the door behind them. "I can't believe someone set out to destroy the statue like that—I bet it is the same person who's been stealing the mail!"

"It's not!" blurted out Ella. "It was . . . it

was *me*! Well, the statue—I haven't been stealing the mail."

"You blew up the statue!" Jess gaped. "What?"

"I didn't mean to." Ella felt awful. "It was supposed to be a birthday surprise for you. The words were supposed to say *Happy Birthday, Jess*."

Jess's mouth opened and closed.

"We were all involved," put in Poppy. "Tilly and I helped make the glitter bomb."

"But it was supposed to be a little bomb—just in here." Tilly gestured around the dorm. "What were you thinking, Ella?"

"I wanted to make it really special!" Ella said. "I wanted to let everyone know it was Jess's birthday and give her a real surprise. I must have put too much powder in."

"Way too much!" said Tilly.

"I'm sorry," said Ella, hot tears prickling her eyes. It had all gone so horribly wrong. "I'm just glad the message didn't work. If it had said *Happy Birthday, Jess*, as it was supposed to, then the Archangel would have guessed right away that it was us."

Jess went over and hugged her. "Oh, Ella." She shook her head. "It was a lovely thought. In fact"—she looked around at the others too—"it's the nicest thing that anyone has ever done for me. But now what are we going to do?"

"I'm going to have to go and admit it was me," said Ella. "I can't let everyone else get into trouble and have the show canceled."

"But you'll be expelled," protested Jess.

"I still have to go and confess," said Ella.

Tears fell down her cheeks. "Maybe I won't be expelled if I go and tell the truth."

"We'll come and take responsibility too," said Poppy.

Tilly nodded. "It is our fault as much as yours."

"No, it's not!" Ella shook her head. "You don't have to come."

"We do. We're all in this together. We're not going to let you take the blame," said Poppy, firmly. She hugged Ella and the other two joined in.

CRASH!

The door was shoved back with a mighty bang. The angels jumped as Primrose entered the room.

"Well, well, well," she sneered. "I suppose you thought no one would realize it was you, but I've guessed exactly what is going on. *Jappy Hirth Bessday*? It's Jess's birthday, isn't it? You told me in assembly," she told Ella. "I reckon you blew up the statue as a surprise. Well, I'm going to go and tell the Archangel right away."

"No, Primrose—no, you mustn't," Jess cried. "Please don't!"

But it was too late. Primrose was already off, flying down the hall.

"Come on!" gasped Jess. "We've got to stop her—before she gets to Archangel Grace!"

CHAPTER 8

An Unexpected Discovery

THE FOUR ANGELS CHARGED DOWN the hallway after Primrose, but she was so good at flying, she raced away from them.

"We've got to catch her!" gasped Poppy. "Ella, you're the fastest of us. You go on ahead!"

Ella beat her wings as fast as she could. She zoomed down the hallway and stairs, through the hall, and out into the courtyard. Primrose had just reached the Archangel and the teachers. "Archangel Grace! Archangel Grace! I know who did it!" Primrose cried in delight.

Archangel Grace and some of the other teachers were clustered around the ruined statue. They seemed to be peering inside. A bluebird was flying around their heads chirping loudly. They all turned.

Primrose's cheeks were flushed and her eyes triumphant. "I know who blew up the statue!" she exclaimed. "It was—"

"Me!" gasped Ella, screeching to a stop beside her.

Primrose looked crestfallen. "Ella wasn't going to admit it!" she told the teachers crossly. "She only came here just now because she knew I'd found out about her plan."

Archangel Grace handed something she was holding to Angel Seraphina. Her eyes were on Ella. "You destroyed the statue, Ella?" she said in astonishment.

Ella nodded. "I'm really, really sorry." The words tumbled out of her. "I didn't mean to blow up the statue. I promise I didn't! And I was coming to tell you, I really was. I didn't

want the fireworks show to be canceled and everyone to be punished because of me." Poppy, Tilly, and Jess landed beside her.

"Ella really was coming to take responsibility," Jess panted.

"I was going to confess too!" said Poppy.

"And me!" said Tilly. "Poppy and I helped Ella make the glitter bomb. It was a birthday surprise to cheer Jess up."

"I wanted it to rain glitter down on her and for everyone to know it was her birthday," said Ella.

"They should all be punished!" said Primrose, smugly.

"It was my idea to put it behind the statue," Ella said, shooting Primrose an angry look. "The others wanted to put it in the dorm. So punish me for destroying the statue, Archangel Grace. Please don't punish them."

"No, it's our fault too!" both Poppy and Tilly protested.

"Ella should be expelled!" Primrose said loudly.

Archangel Grace held up her hands. "Stop! All of you!"

The third graders all fell silent.

"So, let me get this straight," the head teacher said. "Ella, you and Poppy and Tilly made the glitter bomb, but, Ella, you put it behind the statue?"

Ella nodded. "Because I wanted Jess's birthday surprise to be really big. You see, her birthday package hadn't arrived from her parents and . . . and . . ." She suddenly trailed off as she noticed that the teachers around the statue were all holding glittering packages and envelopes. "Packages . . ." She breathed. "There are lots of packages."

Her friends followed her gaze.

"Why have you got so many packages?" said Poppy.

Jess gasped. "That one's from my mom and dad!" She pointed at a sparkly package in Angel Seraphina's hands. "I can see my mom's handwriting on the label."

Angel Seraphina read the label and smiled. "It is indeed for you, Jess—happy birthday." She handed the present to Jess, who promptly opened it.

"A fountain pen!" Jess squealed. "One of those that writes in glitter! And look, it's covered in stars and moons and glitter. *Cherub-azing!*"

Ella blinked. "What's going on?"

Archangel Grace smiled. "Well, Ella, it looks as though you did us a favor by blowing up the statue. We've found our mail thief."

"Who?" all the angels said.

"It was the bluebird," Archangel Grace replied.

"The bluebird!" Ella gasped.

"He must have been nesting inside the hollow statue," said Angel Gabriella, nodding. "Remember how I told you in class that bluebirds like nesting in strange places? Well, this bluebird had clearly decided to nest inside the statue—flying in through Archangel Emmanuel's mouth and nesting in the base."

The bluebird landed on her shoulder and chirped, his head tilted to one side.

"Bluebirds like sparkly things," remembered Ella. "You told us that too."

"Yes, and this one in particular seems to like them. We think he's simply been visiting the pigeonholes in the morning and picking up any packages or cards that caught his attention. Naughty little creature!" Angel Gabriella shook her head.

The bluebird chirped at her boldly.

"So it wasn't an angel after all?" said Ella.

"No, thank goodness, and if you hadn't put your glitter bomb behind the statue, we might never have found out," said Archangel Grace. Her lips twitched into a smile. "Maybe we should be grateful to you, Ella Brown."

"Grateful!" spluttered Primrose. "Ella should be punished, Archangel. She's broken the statue—"

"Primrose, that's enough! The statue can be fixed with magic. Besides, aren't you forgetting who the head teacher is here?" Archangel Grace said very sharply. Primrose subsided. "So,

Ella . . ." Archangel Grace turned to Ella again. "The question is, what should we do with you?"

Ella hung her head. What was her punishment going to be?

"What you did was clearly wrong, but it was obviously an accident," Archangel Grace said. "You were doing it for your friend, to cheer her up, and that shows real angel qualities. You have also demonstrated a real aptitude for glitter bomb making. Hmm . . ." She pressed her fingers together and regarded Ella. "Let me see. . . ."

"I really am very sorry," Ella said contritely. "I promise I'll never do it again."

Archangel Grace's eyes twinkled. "Then I think, my dear, we'll say no more about it."

"You mean I'm not going to be expelled?" Ella burst out in relief.

"No, no expulsions today," Archangel Grace said.

"I won't even take a halo stamp away, as you were trying to help a friend," Archangel Grace said, "but I will have to punish you. Weeding—the whole of the vegetable patch—and by bedtime this evening."

Ella nodded. She knew that it was more than fair.

"I'll help you," Tilly whispered, before turning to Archangel Grace. "So the fireworks show can definitely go ahead tomorrow?"

"It can indeed," said Archangel Grace. "In fact, maybe Ella would like to make another bomb, seeing as she is so good at it—only with Angel Gabriella's help this time. It can go off right at the end, as our final climax, after Primrose has performed. It seems a pity to waste such talent."

"But Archangel Grace, that's not fair! Ella really should lose a halo stamp as well for what she's done," cried Primrose.

Archangel Grace smiled and ruffled Primrose's hair. "Oh, Primrose, you heard what I said. Ella's going to weed the whole vegetable patch. That's quite enough. Besides, I think we've had enough excitement for one day." The head teacher paused. "Don't you?"

Ella looked up in the sky the next evening. Whizzes and bangs filled the air and flashes of light zoomed across the night. All of the third-grade angels were great in the show. As they whizzed back and forth with the lights there were oohs and aahs from the crowd. The third graders' glitter bombs were mounted on trees for the finale, and with Angel Gabriella conducting, the third graders all waved their wands and counted to three. The bombs exploded, sending glitter and sparkles high into the sky. Ella flew to the side and waited to set off the massive glitter bomb she and Angel Gabriella had made that afternoon. It was going to be the very last thing in the show. First, Primrose had to appear in her starring role.

"I can't believe you're in the finale with me!" Primrose hissed by her side. "You should have been sent home. You should have been expelled . . ."

Ella just smiled to herself. She was so delighted by the show that even Primrose wasn't going to make her lose her temper that evening.

"You and your friends are never going to get enough halo stamps to even get sapphire halos, let alone make it to Guardian Angels. You—"

"Primrose . . . Primrose . . . Come on, or you'll miss your moment!" called Angel Celestine.

Ella giggled as Primrose rushed forward. She'd been so busy being horrible that she'd nearly missed her cue!

Primrose was clearly flustered, and as she flew through the sky, she got into a complete mess, missing the hoops of light that she was supposed to fly through.

There was a silence, and then the crowd clapped half-heartedly but there was no rousing cheer. Primrose stormed off past Ella with a face like thunder.

"Oh dear, that wasn't a very impressive end to our show. I hope you can do better, Ella." Angel Celestine pushed Ella on. "Show everyone what the third-grade angels can do!"

Ella felt the butterflies in her stomach as she flitted forward with the glitter bomb in her arms, but once she was out there, she forgot everything and flew across the sky, making the perfect loop-the-loop.

"Hooray!" The cries echoed in her ears.

It was now or never. Ella threw the glitter ball up as high as she could. It soared into the air. Ella waved her wand three times and counted down. "One ... two ... three!" she shouted.

BANG!

The bomb exploded in the sky and the words formed in glittery pinks and purples.

There was a roar from the crowd. Ella smiled.

She paused for a moment to look down at all of the happy faces beneath her, before gently coming down to land beside her family and friends to the sound of rapturous

applause. It was so good to see her parents again and she gave them a big hug. Poppy, Jess, and Tilly were doing the same to theirs. It was so lovely to see them all so happy, especially Tilly, who had been so homesick at the start of the term.

"Ella . . . Ella, that was fabulous." Her mother hugged her.

Her dad looked on proudly. "Who would have thought it?" he said. "My little Ella, the star of the show. My perfect angel."

Ella looked across at her friends. Tilly and Poppy raised their eyebrows and Jess chuckled. If only Ella's parents knew the truth! But they didn't say anything.

Ella left her parents for a moment to give her friends a big hug.

"We did it!" they cheered. "Hip, hip, hooray! We really did it. Now we get to go home for the break too!"

"And then we'll be back at angel school for a lot more adventures—and to try and earn our sapphire halos," grinned Ella. "I can't wait!"

Secrets and Sapphires

For Saskia Ramsey,
with love

CHAPTER 1

New Halos!

"HAVE YOU HEARD THE NEWS?" whispered Ella Brown in excitement, as she sat down next to her friend Poppy in morning assembly.

"What news?" Poppy demanded.

"It's angel-tastic! Someone in our year has . . ."

"Shh!" Tilly, one of their other friends, hushed them hastily. She nodded to the stage where Archangel Grace, the head of the

Guardian Angel Academy, was waiting for silence. Archangel Grace was a plump angel with wise eyes, enormous gossamer wings, and dark hair that was pulled back into a bun on the back of her head.

Ella fidgeted in frustration on the bench. She was longing to tell Poppy what she had just overheard on the way into the hall but she didn't want to be scolded by Archangel Grace. She pushed her shoulder-length brown hair behind her ears and tried to concentrate.

"Good morning, angels," Archangel Grace said, smiling around at the school. "Now, before I make the morning announcements, I have some good news." She paused. "A third-grade angel has just completed her first halo card!"

"That's what I was going to tell you!"

hissed Ella, elbowing Poppy in the ribs, as excited gasps filled the air.

"Who is it?" whispered Poppy eagerly.

"I don't know!" Ella replied. All the angels at the academy had a halo card and were awarded halo stamps for good behavior. When an angel's halo card was completely filled in, the angel's halo would change color and her wings grow bigger. The white halos all the angels started with changed to sapphire, which changed to ruby and so on, all the way up until the final level was reached—the diamond level. Only the very best, most angelic angels ever got a diamond halo. Ella longed to have one.

She looked at the rest of the third graders, sitting on the bench. They all had white halos at the moment. Which of them had filled in their card? She knew that it wasn't one of her best friends. Poppy, whose messy blonde curls were half hanging out of her ponytail and whose white dress was covered in splotches of ink, was lovely, but she was very clumsy and untidy—neither of which were perfect angel qualities. Tilly and Jess found it easier to get halo stamps—they were both quieter and more well-behaved—but Ella knew Jess needed another four halo stamps and Tilly another two. Ella touched her own halo card in her pocket and sighed.

One thing was for sure—it definitely wasn't her. She still had ten halo stamps to get!

Halo stamps were awarded for being good and doing kind deeds, and although Ella liked to think she was kind, she definitely wasn't always good! She just couldn't help herself. She always tried her hardest, but somehow she couldn't stop herself from getting into trouble!

"Olivia Starfall, would you like to come up here?" Archangel Grace called over to where a sweet-looking angel with long dark hair and bright-blue eyes was sitting, a little ways from Ella, her ankles crossed and her hands folded neatly in her lap.

Olivia! Of course! Ella wasn't surprised as Olivia stood up, blushing. Olivia was wonderful—always happy to help out if you got stuck, but modest too. She could fly the most perfect loop-the-loop, her silver linings were careful and tidy, and her hair neatly combed. Ella smiled and applauded with the others when Olivia flew up to the stage, her tiny wings fluttering.

As she landed beside Archangel Grace, all of the angels cheered loudly. Well, nearly all of them—Ella caught sight of another angel at the far end of the third-grade bench who didn't look pleased at all. With her golden hair curled into ringlets, big blue eyes, and spotless uniform, you would have thought she was a perfect angel, if it wasn't for the scowl on her face. Primrose!

As Primrose leaned in to whisper to the red-haired angel beside her, she covered her mouth with her hand and her eyes narrowed spitefully. Ella sighed. She was sure that Primrose wasn't saying anything nice about Olivia. Ella turned back. Olivia was standing next to Archangel Grace now, her face pink with embarrassment. Archangel Grace raised her wand.

"Good shall be rewarded, virtue too, white halo change to shining blue . . ." She waved her wand in the air three times and a small cloud of glittering silver angel dust cascaded down from it, landing on Olivia's halo. Instantly it turned to deep . glowing sapphire, and Olivia's white uniform became the pale blue of a spring sky.

A chorus of gasps and sighs filled the room.

"Wow, isn't that amazing!"

"She looks really beautiful!"

"Oh, I remember getting my sapphire halo when I was a third grader!"

Ella fluttered her own tiny little wings. She wanted to be up on that stage so badly. "I hope I get a sapphire halo soon," she breathed.

As Olivia flew back to her place,

Archangel Grace called for silence again. "And now, on to another matter. A rather less happy one. As you all know, we make our very own angel dust here at the school. It comes from glitter flowers, which are very rare, and it has come to my attention that we're very low on stock. We've planted a new crop of flowers in the school greenhouse, but it will take some time before they bloom. Isn't that right, Angel Celestine?" Archangel Grace turned to a pretty, dark-haired teacher who was seated with the other teachers at the back of the stage.

"It is indeed," said Angel Celestine, the gardening teacher. "The crop needs to flower before the glitter can be harvested, which can be tricky. Conditions need to be just right.

Hopefully, we should be able to renew our supply of angel dust soon."

Archangel Grace nodded. "And in the meantime, the remaining angel dust must be used sparingly. As you all know, we were going to have the school Spring Picnic next weekend, but I'm going to have to cancel it for the time being to save on magic."

"Oh no . . ." There were groans from around the room.

Ella had never actually been to the Spring Picnic but she'd heard all about it and had been looking forward to it too. Disappointment flooded through her.

Archangel Grace held up her hands again and silence fell. "I know that this will be a huge disappointment to you, and I'm really sorry for that, but I am sure you can all understand that we must be sensible. If we run out of angel dust, we won't be able to do any angel magic, and that would be a catastrophe."

The angels in the room nodded understandingly.

"We will have the picnic when the flowers can be harvested," said Archangel Grace. "In the meantime, if anyone would like to help out in the greenhouses, looking after the plants, then I am sure Angel Celestine would be very grateful. Now let us all stand and sing *Glad Tidings and Silver Linings.*"

When assembly was over, Ella filed out of the hall with the other angels. As soon as they were away from the teachers' watchful eyes, she crowded around with her friends.

"Isn't it amazing about Olivia?" Tilly burst out.

"Just glittersome!" said Poppy.

"It'll be us next," Jess joined in, flicking her long dark ponytail over her shoulder.

"Well, maybe you and Tilly." Ella sighed. "But Poppy and I have quite a few more halo stamps to get, don't we, Poppy?"

But Poppy wasn't listening. She was looking at the other side of the room where Primrose was now standing with her arm linked through Olivia's. "Primrose is unbelievable," she said, shaking her head. "Yesterday she made a fuss because she didn't want to sit with Olivia in forgetting spell class because she said Olivia was boring. Now she's acting like they're best friends!"

Primrose simpered as people came up to congratulate the other girl. "Oh, I always knew darling Livvy would be the first to get her sapphire halo," she said loudly. "She's wonderful, isn't she?"

Olivia gave Primrose a very surprised look.

Ella snorted. "If getting a sapphire halo means having Primrose hanging around, then maybe I don't want to fill my halo card after all."

"Shh! They're coming over!" hissed Jess.

Olivia headed in their direction, with Primrose holding tightly to her arm.

"Congratulations, Olivia." Ella smiled.

"Thanks, Ella," said Olivia shyly. "I can't believe I was the first to get my sapphire halo. It was a real fluke."

"I was just saying how amazing Olivia's sapphire dress and halo look on her, don't you agree?" Primrose gushed. "It's cherub-azing!"

"Er, thank you," said Olivia, clearly flustered by Primrose's attention. "Well, I've got to get something from my dorm. I'll . . . um, see you later." She managed to extract herself from Primrose's grasp and hurried away.

"Don't be long! I'll save you a seat in class!" Primrose called sweetly after her.

"What's going on, Primrose?" Ella demanded. "Since when have you saved Olivia a seat in class?"

Primrose gave her a wide-eyed look. "I'm just being thoughtful."

"Thoughtful!" spluttered Ella. "You've never said two words to Olivia before, but suddenly she gets a sapphire halo and you're her new best friend. I bet you just want to hang around with her now because everyone's giving her lots of attention."

"What a mean thing to say!" Primrose looked shocked. "And when I was only trying to do a kind deed. You know the school handbook says perfect angels are always kind."

She gave Ella a snooty look. "Though why I should expect you to know anything about being the perfect angel, I don't know. How many halo stamps do you still have to get before your card is full, Ella? Is it five? Six? Oh, sorry, I think it's ten, isn't it? Ten!" She rolled her eyes. "And I need . . . hmm, just four. Well, never mind. I'm sure you'll complete your first halo card one day—even if the rest of us have our diamond halos by then! Now, please excuse me or I will be late for class."

Putting her nose in the air, she flew away.

Ella let out a frustrated exclamation. "Halos and wings! Primrose is so annoying!"

"Calm down," said Tilly, putting a hand soothingly on Ella's arm. "She's not worth getting upset over."

"Definitely not," declared Poppy. "You'll fill your halo card up quickly. We all will. Who cares who gets there first?"

"Soon we'll all have sapphire halos like Olivia," said Jess happily. "But Primrose was right about one thing—we'd better not be late for Angel Gabriella or we'll lose some of the halo stamps we've already got!"

"Come on!" Ella cried, whizzing into the air. "Let's go!"

CHAPTER 2

Phoenix Fun!

C HEEP . . . "

Ella pushed back the door to the heavenly animals class to see the smallest, sweetest golden bird sitting on a perch in the middle of the room. Angel Gabriella, their teacher, was standing next to it, gently stroking its feathers.

"Shush . . . quietly," she mouthed the words as Ella and her friends flew in.

"He's a phoenix chick," she explained as they gathered around the table with the other angels. Primrose was already standing there with Olivia. Veronica, Primrose's best friend, was standing to one side looking upset as Primrose whispered to Olivia and giggled with her. Olivia's own best friend, Susie, looked a bit fed up too. Ella saw her edging over to Veronica.

Ella stared at the baby bird. She'd heard about the phoenix—it was a rare, magical bird who laid an egg in a fire when it came to the end of its life and then was reborn from the egg. But she'd never met one. "What's he doing here?" she breathed.

"He's just hatched out of his egg. His name's Jewel," said Angel Gabriella. "I thought you could all draw him. You're used to copying magical animals from books, but what makes an angel a real artist is if she can draw from the real thing."

"Cheep . . . ," the baby phoenix called again, as if agreeing with Angel Gabriella, before stretching out his wings and settling down. The little crest on the top of his head wobbled. It looked like a tiny crown.

"He's so cute!" said Jess.

"Can I hold him?" asked Poppy longingly.

"Maybe later," said Angel Gabriella. "But for now could you all stand back a little bit?

I don't want you to crowd him. Can you see how he's starting to change color?"

Ella looked. The phoenix had indeed changed color—the tips of his golden feathers had flushed a ruby red.

"That's because he's feeling frightened," Angel Gabriella explained. "The more frightened he is, the deeper red his feathers will become. We need to put him at ease." She stroked him again, and as the girls stepped farther away, his feathers settled back down to pure gold. "It's really important to look after all creatures, great and small," Angel Gabriella explained. "That's an important part of being an angel."

"I've always been good at looking after animals and birds, Angel Gabriella," Primrose joined in smugly. "At home we found a baby bluebird once. It had dropped out of its nest. I fed him bread and milk every day until he was better."

Ella raised her eyebrows. Primrose had never shown any interest in animals they'd met in heavenly creatures class. It was probably her mother who had looked after the bluebird. If there had even been a bluebird and it wasn't just a made-up story.

"That was very caring of you, Primrose." Angel Gabriella nodded.

"Do I get a halo stamp?" asked Primrose hopefully.

"Not quite yet, Primrose," Angel Gabriella said, laughing. "Though you get marks for trying!"

"I helped a unicorn too once," Primrose went on. "He stayed at my house for weeks and weeks even after he was better. He was just like a great big pet."

"But, Angel Gabriella, aren't you supposed to release animals back into the wild quickly?" Ella asked. She really did know about animals. She had helped a baby fawn out in the woods near her parents' house once and looked after a rabbit with a broken leg. She had pet fish, too—sparkly ones that lived in a magical orb in her room.

"That's very true, Ella," said Angel Gabriella. "If an animal is wild, as soon as they're ready to go, we free them. It's better for them that way. We'll talk more about that later, but for now we've got to get on with our life drawing. Everyone, sit at your desks."

The little phoenix settled down again onto the perch in the middle of the table as all of the angels went to their desks.

Ella sat next to Poppy, took out her box of paints from her bag, and placed them carefully by her side before laying out her brushes. But first she had to sketch. As the pencil moved across the paper, she lost herself in her drawing. She looked up for a moment. Poppy was chewing on the end of her pencil. Ella buried herself back in her work. It wasn't until she had nearly drawn the whole phoenix that she stopped and looked up again.

"That's very good, Ella," said Angel Gabriella, coming to a stop beside her. "You've always been really good at copying, but it's a real art to be able to draw from life, too. And you've done it so quickly."

"Thank you, Angel Gabriella." Ella smiled, feeling the pride swell up inside her.

"Let's see, Ella," called Poppy. "Turn it around."

Ella did as Poppy had asked.

Poppy grinned. "It's wonderful—but then your drawings always are!"

Angel Gabriella smiled at her. "You can have a halo stamp for being generous with your praise, Poppy. And, Ella, you can have one for doing such a good drawing. Take your cards to Archangel Grace's office when you have a moment, girls, and she'll give you your stamps."

Poppy and Ella exchanged delighted looks. Halo stamps were even better when they were totally unexpected! Across the room, Primrose looked fed up. "Angel Gabriella! Come and look at my picture! I've half-finished it!" she called. Angel Gabriella went over.

"So, let's see what you've done," said Ella to Poppy.

"I haven't actually drawn anything yet," admitted Poppy. "I'm not ready. I think I need to take a closer look at Jewel first."

She jumped up, almost tripping over Ella's bag in the process, and went over to the table where the phoenix was. Ella went back to her work. She was so busy that when an alarmed cheep and flapping of wings filled the air, she didn't really notice. But then there was a cry.

"Oh no, what have I done?" Poppy wailed.

Ella looked up quickly. Jewel was on the floor with Poppy crouching beside him.

"What's happened here?" said Angel Gabriella, hurrying over.

"It was Poppy!" cried out Primrose. "I saw her! Poppy dropped Jewel!"

"Did you? Oh, Poppy!" Angel Gabriella swooped down and picked up Jewel. She examined him, carefully laying out each wing and leg while Poppy watched, her face pale. Finally Angel Gabriella put him back on the table with a sigh of relief. "Well, he seems to be unharmed. What were you thinking of, Poppy? Why did you pick him up?"

"I didn't mean to drop him." Poppy hung her head. "I just wanted to have a closer look, and he seemed happy, but then he wriggled and flapped his wings . . . and . . . and . . . Oh, why am I so clumsy!"

"Never mind this time," said Angel Gabriella. "Thankfully there's no harm done, but that's why I was saying earlier you have to be so careful with animals. You could have really hurt him. Do you understand?"

"I do, and I'm so very sorry, Angel Gabriella," said Poppy contritely.

"Then we'll say no more about it," said Angel Gabriella. "Now, how far have you gotten with your picture?"

"Not very far." Poppy bit her lip. "In fact, I . . . I haven't even started."

Angel Gabriella sighed. "And class is almost over now. You'll have to stay inside during break to finish it."

"Of course, Angel Gabriella," Poppy said. She walked sadly back to Ella.

"Don't worry. I'll stay and help you, Poppy," Ella whispered.

"That's very kind of you, Ella," said Angel Gabriella who had overheard, although Ella hadn't meant her to. "And for that I'm going to award you a second halo stamp."

"I could stay and help too," Primrose joined in hastily.

"Thank you, Primrose," said Angel Gabriella. "But I think one angel helping Poppy is quite enough."

"I didn't mean I would help Poppy,"

Primrose said. "But my friend hasn't finished her picture yet either. Veronica . . . Veronica," she called across to the desk where Veronica was sitting. "You haven't finished, have you?"

"Yes, I have," said Veronica, looking puzzled.

"No you haven't," said Primrose, going over to her.

At that moment, Jewel let out a little cheep, and Angel Gabriella was distracted. Quickly, Primrose pulled an eraser out of her pocket and erased a little bit of Veronica's picture.

"Hey!" cried Veronica.

"Shush," said Primrose, placing a neat little white ballet slipper on Veronica's foot to stop her from saying anything.

"Ouch—that hurts!" Veronica spluttered.

"What was that, Veronica?" Angel Gabriella turned back to the class.

Primrose gave Veronica a sharp look.

"Nothing, Angel Gabriella," Veronica said meekly.

"Okay, now where was I?" Angel Gabriella said. "Oh yes, Veronica . . . Primrose was saying you needed to stay and finish your picture too. Is that right?"

"Yes, Angel Gabriella." Veronica sighed.

"Remember that I said I'd stay and help her," Primrose reminded Angel Gabriella.

"Oh yes, yes," Angel Gabriella said distractedly. "That's very kind."

"So, do I get a halo stamp too?" asked Primrose eagerly.

"Well," Angel Gabriella hesitated. "You're not really supposed to get them for asking, but I suppose on this occasion, it's all right. Primrose, one halo stamp for you as well."

Primrose waited until the teacher had turned away and then flashed Ella a smug look.

"Great!" Ella muttered under her breath to Poppy. "Now we have to put up with Primrose during break time too!"

In no time at all, the classroom was cleared, and soon it was just Ella, Poppy, Veronica, and Primrose left in the heavenly animals classroom with Angel Gabriella putting her things away. Ella could see that Poppy was still upset about Jewel, and she wanted to cheer her up. She picked up a pencil and balanced it on her upper lip.

"Look!" she whispered, nudging her. Poppy giggled, so Ella did it again, moving her lip and making the pencil move up and down like a mustache.

"Stop it, Ella," said Poppy, trying to ignore her. "I'll never get this finished."

Ella took the pencil and pulled a loose thread off her dress. She tied it onto the end of the pencil like a tail and put the pencil back on her upper lip again.

"Now what are you doing?" Poppy hissed, glancing over.

Ella grinned. "It's a mouse-tache!"

Poppy snorted with laughter. Angel Gabriella looked around. Quickly, Ella stopped what she was doing, but it was too late. The teacher had caught her with the pencil on her lip. Ella groaned inwardly, waiting to be scolded, but Angel Gabriella simply shook her head and smiled.

"I'm not even going to ask you what you're doing, Ella. You know, you might not be the most angelic angel, and you might not have the most halo stamps, but life would certainly be a lot more boring without you around!"

Ella felt taken aback. "What do you mean, Angel Gabriella? Angel Gabriella . . ."

But Angel Gabriella had already left the room. Ella turned to look at Poppy, wondering what her friend had made of the comment, but Poppy was still busy trying to finish her picture. Ella rubbed her forehead. She knew she wasn't a perfect angel, but she wasn't sure she really liked hearing a teacher say it out loud. What exactly had Angel Gabriella meant by it? Had she meant it in a nice way, or had she been scolding her? Maybe she thought Ella would never be a perfect angel?

Primrose flew over. "See, even the teachers know you're a bad angel!" she whispered.

"They know you'll never get a diamond halo. I bet they think you won't even get a sapphire one!"

Ella jumped to her feet and glared at Primrose. But Primrose was already flying swiftly toward the door. "I'm going now!" she called to Veronica.

"What about helping me?" protested Veronica.

Primrose shrugged. "You're almost done. You can finish it on your own. I'm going to get my halo stamp from Archangel Grace."

Ella watched her go. Her mouth felt dry. She knew Primrose was just being mean, but maybe she was right. Maybe her teachers did think she'd never make it to guardian angel level.

"Ella, can you help me draw the wings?" Poppy asked.

"Of course," Ella said, turning her attention to Poppy and the drawing. She tried to forget Primrose's comment, but no matter how hard she pushed it away, it just wouldn't leave her mind. . . .

CHAPTER 3

A Special Guest

AS SOON AS POPPY HAD FINISHED her drawing, they went outside. Tilly and Jess had told them that they were going to spend break time helping in the greenhouses, so they went to find them.

The greenhouses were at the bottom of the garden next to a few small wooden toolsheds. They were very large and ornate, and their panes of glass sparkled in the sun. Ella and Poppy started flying across the grass when they saw Jess and Tilly hurrying over.

"Look! They're carrying something." Ella turned to Poppy. "What is it?"

"I don't know," said Poppy. "But it looks fluffy."

Sure enough, as they got closer, they could see that Jess had an animal in her arms—a brown fluffy bundle with two long ears and a twitchy nose. It had a white chest and pretty white markings on its back in the shape of stars.

"What is it?" Ella called, flying down.

"A celestial bunny," Jess said breathlessly. "We found him over by the greenhouse just when we were about to go in. He's a baby one. He's been hurt."

The little animal's ears moved back and forth and his long whiskers trembled.

"He was really scared when we found him," Tilly said breathlessly. "So I used a calming spell. He's still a bit anxious, but at least he let us pick him up."

"That was a really good idea to use a spell like that," said Ella.

"We used a healing spell too," said Jess. "His paw was bleeding. It's stopped now but the wound is still there."

Ella nodded. Now that she looked, she

noticed that Jess had a few spots of blood on her white dress. "We should get him inside," she said. "Let's find Angel Seraphina. She'll know what to do."

"Good idea," said Poppy. Their class tutor was always full of good ideas.

They hurried back toward the school. As they went in through the back door, they bumped into Primrose coming down the staircase from Archangel Grace's study.

"What have you got there?" she exclaimed and broke off. "Ew!" she squealed dramatically. "Is that blood on your dress, Jess?"

"It's only a few spots," said Jess. "We found an injured bunny. We managed to heal the wound."

"Yuck!" Primrose shuddered.

"Have you seen Angel Seraphina?" Poppy asked Primrose.

"No. Why do you want her?"

Ella stared at her. "Maybe for this hurt bunny?"

"Can't you just let it go in the gardens?" said Primrose. "It's only a silly little bunny."

"No we can't just let it go!" Ella said crossly. "It's been hurt."

"I wonder where Angel Seraphina is," said Tilly anxiously.

"Did I hear my name, girls?"

Ella breathed a huge sigh of relief as a beautiful young guardian angel came flying along the corridor, her gossamer wings gleaming, her halo shining with diamonds.

"Angel Seraphina . . . you've got to help.

Tilly and Jess found a bunny . . . a baby one," Ella said breathlessly. "He's been hurt— his paw was bleeding. We've used a calming spell to calm him and a healing one for his

paw," she explained. "Or rather Tilly and Jess did," she said, anxious not to take the credit for something she hadn't done.

"That was quick thinking, angels," said Angel Seraphina. "Let me take a look. . . ."

Jess released her hold on the bunny, and, startled, it leaped into Angel Seraphina's arms. Angel Seraphina stroked the little creature and started to check him over.

"You did well to use the healing spell," she said. "The paw's already on the mend. If you hadn't acted so quickly, he would have lost quite a lot of blood."

The baby bunny looked a little less startled now, Angel Seraphina's voice was so calming. Its nostrils had stopped twitching as it started to relax.

"Three halo stamps each, Tilly and Jess," said Angel Seraphina.

"Three halo stamps?" said Tilly, surprised.

"Three WHOLE halo stamps?" Primrose exclaimed. "Just for looking after a bunny!"

"Yes, Primrose . . ." Angel Seraphina looked at the angel in surprise.

"But—" Primrose went to speak, but Angel Seraphina held up her hand to silence her and turned back to Jess and Tilly.

"You can collect your halo stamps from Archangel Grace later," she said. "Right now we need to deal with this baby bunny. He'll need to rest for a week before we release him, just to make sure he's healthy and well enough to survive in the wild. He'll need looking after while he's staying with us. Would any of you be kind enough to volunteer?"

"Me ... Me! I'll look after him!" Primrose broke in, even before the final word was out of Angel Seraphina's mouth.

Ella looked surprised. Only five minutes ago, Primrose had wanted to let the bunny go in the garden. She also felt a flash of real disappointment. She would have loved to have looked after the sweet little creature.

"Please, please, please, Angel Seraphina," Primrose pleaded. "I'll take really good care of him."

Angel Seraphina smiled. "Thank you, Primrose. And a halo stamp for volunteering."

"Glittersome!" cried Primrose. "Just two more stamps to go!"

"All right, Primrose," said Angel Seraphina, looking slightly displeased. "That's quite enough. What happened to the golden angel rule—*angels must never show off*?"

Primrose looked embarrassed. "I'm sorry, Angel Seraphina," she apologized meekly.

"That's all right, my dear. Now, do we have a name for this bunny?" Angel Seraphina started again.

"Star," burst out Ella, who'd been thinking

about it while they'd been talking. She reached out and stroked his fur. "I think he should be called Star after the markings on his back."

"Very good." Angel Seraphina nodded. "Star it is." She let Ella hold him and give him a cuddle. "Now, I've got a class to get to, so, Primrose, why don't you take Star out into the gardens. There's a potting shed over by the greenhouse that should make a nice home for him. It's quiet and cozy and there's plenty of hay nearby. You'll find a spare hutch in there too."

"Of course. I'll take him there right away, Angel Seraphina," Primrose said.

And that was that. As the teacher swept out of the room, Tilly, Poppy, and Jess followed her, leaving Ella and Primrose alone in the room together. Primrose made as if to leave as well.

"Er, aren't you forgetting something, Primrose?" Ella said quickly.

"What?" said Primrose.

"Four legs, two ears, a twitchy nose . . . something you've just promised to take care of, remember?" Ella held out the bunny.

"Oh, him." Primrose looked disgruntled.

"Yes, Star! Whatever happened to all the 'please, please, please,'" Ella went on, doing a pretty good impression of Primrose's voice.

"All right, all right." Gingerly, Primrose went to take Star from Ella. She hesitated.

"What's wrong?" said Ella.

"It's just, well, won't his claws scratch my dress?"

"Oh for goodness' sake, Primrose." Ella rolled her eyes. "I'll carry him to the shed if you're worried about that."

She cuddled the bunny close and gave him a little scratch behind his ears. His dark eyes gazed trustingly at her. "Come on, Star," she whispered. "Let's get you settled into your new home. . . ."

CHAPTER 4

Sparkling Sapphire

ELLA HURRIED OUT IN THE DIRECTION of the greenhouse with Primrose following. "I don't know why you said you would look after Star if you don't even want to carry him," Ella said. "Did you really only offer so you could get a halo stamp?"

"What's it to you, anyway?" said Primrose haughtily.

Ella cuddled the baby bunny. "I'd have looked after him even if I hadn't gotten any halo stamps for it. Look, why don't you let me care for him, Primrose?"

"No! Then you will get halo stamps!"

Ella only just held on to her temper. She felt like shouting at Primrose, but she'd had halo stamps taken away in the past when she had become angry with the other angel and she wasn't about to risk that again. Not when everyone was so close to getting their sapphire halos.

"Fine," she said abruptly. "Just make sure you look after him well." She kissed the top of Star's head and felt him nestle closer.

They carried on in silence and rounded the corner. The potting shed lay there before them. Ella pushed back the door and stepped inside. It was warm and inviting. Rays of sunlight slanted in through the small window and there was a hutch in one corner, as well as some bags of hay and straw and food. "Can you get the hutch ready while I hold him?" Ella said.

Wrinkling her nose in distaste, Primrose pulled some hay from the bag and started putting it into the main bit of hutch. "No!" Ella stopped her. "The straw goes in there, not the hay. He eats the hay. Haven't you ever looked after an animal like a bunny before?"

"Of course I have!" said Primrose. She shoved the straw and hay in haphazardly. "All done. Put him in."

"Um . . . and what about some water? And food?" Ella said. She saw Primrose's blank look. "Okay, okay, I'll do it." Gently, she put

Star inside the hutch, spreading out the straw into an inviting thick bed with one hand and soothing him with the other. Then she shut the door, filled the water bottle, and put some of the dry food in a little dish.

"This will do for him for now, but he really needs vegetables, too, like carrots and cabbage. Will you make sure you get him some from the gardens?" said Ella.

"Mmm," Primrose said distractedly as she examined her reflection in a little gold hand mirror. "Sure, sure. I'll get whatever he needs."

Ella wasn't convinced. The bunny looked at her and twitched his nose. "You know that he needs feeding three times a day?"

"Yep," Primrose said, inspecting her face and twining a curl around one finger.

"And his water needs changing every day," said Ella.

"Uh-huh," said Primrose.

"And he needs lots of cuddling," said Ella.

"Yes, all right, I get it," Primrose said crossly, snapping her mirror shut. "Now can you leave me alone? I said I'd look after him, didn't I?"

"Okay." Ella hesitated. She was reluctant to leave Primrose, but Angel Seraphina had given Primrose the job, so there really wasn't anything she could do. She shouldn't interfere. . . .

Ella flew slowly back in the direction of the Guardian Angel Academy. She couldn't stop thinking about Star. She hated leaving Primrose to look after him. *I'll make sure I keep an eye on her,* she thought. She was so deep in thought that when she reached the door to the Academy, she didn't notice another angel flying out.

"Angels and wings! Watch out, Ella!"

It was Jess!

"Whoops, sorry, Jess," Ella said. "I was miles away." She realized her friend had a massive beam on her face. "You look happy."

"Oh, I am! So happy!" said Jess. "I was just coming to look for you. Come quickly . . . Tilly's got something to show you. She's in the common room. You've got to see it!"

"See what?" Ella said, puzzled.

"I can't believe you haven't realized," said Jess, giggling. "Come on!" She raced back into the school with Ella flying after her. They flew down the maze of hallways before arriving at a door. Ella pushed it back . . . and stopped in her tracks.

"Tilly!" she gasped.

There in front of Ella stood her friend, but instead of her usual pearly white dress, she was head to toe in pale blue and her halo glittered with sapphires!

"Do you like it?" Tilly did a little twirl.

"I've just come back from Archangel Grace's study."

For a moment, Ella couldn't do anything but gape. "Oh . . . w-w-wow!" she stammered. Of course—those extra three halo stamps for helping Star would have filled Tilly's halo card. Ella was overwhelmed with emotions. She was delighted for Tilly, but at the same time, deep down, she felt a stab of jealousy and worry. Tilly had gotten her sapphire halo! Jess would be next. Then Poppy.

What about me? she thought as Angel Gabriella's words came back to her. *What if I never get my sapphire halo?*

Tilly looked at her expectantly. Ella realized she was waiting for her to say something. In fact, so were Jess and Poppy.

"You look, um . . . angel-tastic," she said with a weak smile. Even to her ears she didn't sound very convincing.

Tilly's smile faded slightly. "What's wrong?"

"Nothing," Ella said quickly.

"I thought you'd be really happy for Tilly," Jess said.

"I am!" Ella nodded hard, trying to sound convincing. "Totally and utterly, completely happy. It's really glittery, Tilly." She swallowed, fighting back the jealousy inside. "Good job." She turned hastily away. "I need to get something from the dorm."

"Ella?" Poppy said.

But Ella quickly flew away.

"What's up with Ella?" she heard Jess say.

"Maybe it's this new uniform. Maybe it doesn't look good on me?" she heard Tilly say uncertainly.

Ella blocked her ears and flew on.

"Ella! Wait!" Poppy came after her. Ella pretended not to hear. She was better at flying than Poppy and she zoomed on ahead.

"Ella!"

Poppy was panting by the time she caught up with Ella at the dorm door, and her blond curls were even messier than usual. "Okay, what's going on? I know you heard me back there. Why didn't you wait? And why were you so strange with Tilly?"

Ella opened the door and hurried inside the dorm. It looked just as pretty as ever with their rainbow-colored cloud beds floating in the air and a golden dove cooing from above the door. A large oval window looked out on to the grounds. Ella went over to the window and gazed out of it.

"Ella?"

"Don't you care that Tilly has her sapphire halo and we don't?" Ella burst out, swinging around.

Poppy looked at her in astonishment. "Why should I care about that? Tilly's a much better angel than I am. I always knew she would get her sapphire halo before me."

Ella sighed. She knew that what Poppy was saying made sense—it just made her feel all the more terrible for feeling jealous and not being nicer to Tilly back in the common room.

"It's not a competition, Ella," Poppy said softly. "We'll all get a sapphire halo in the end if we try hard enough."

Ella nodded slowly. "You're so much nicer than me," she said miserably. "I'm an awful angel!"

"No you're not," said Poppy, giving her a

big hug. "You're honest, that's all. And that's an important angel quality too, remember? Angel Seraphina's always saying that."

Poppy's words were a huge comfort, but Ella still felt bad. Poppy wasn't jealous, so why should she be? She really was a terrible friend and a terrible angel. *It'll be Jess who gets a sapphire halo next*, an anxious little voice in her head said. Then Poppy. *I'll be the only one with a white one.*

"Come on, let's go back and find the others," said Poppy.

Ella took a deep breath and followed her slowly out the door.

CHAPTER 5

A Discovery

ELLA TRIED VERY HARD TO BE HAPPY for Tilly over the next few days, but the jealous feelings wouldn't go away. She felt really bad about it. A good angel wouldn't ever have such horrible feelings, she was sure. It made her much quieter than usual. Luckily, her friends were busy and didn't notice too much. They were all helping out in the greenhouses with the glitter plants whenever they could—watering them, giving them flower food, making sure they

were turned regularly so that their leaves all got an equal amount of sun. Everyone in the school wanted the plants to flower so that the glitter dust supplies could be renewed—and so that the Spring Picnic could happen!

Unfortunately, Angel Celestine couldn't tell them exactly when that would be. Apparently, all you could do was care for the plants and wait for conditions to be exactly right and then the flowering would begin.

Jess, Tilly, and Poppy loved helping in the greenhouses, and went every break and at lunchtime, but Ella wasn't so excited. She thought plants were boring. Whenever they went to the greenhouses she would look at the little potting shed where Star was being kept and wish she could be looking after him instead. But whenever she tried to go in and see him, she found that the door was locked. Strangely, she never seemed to see Primrose there, but a few days after Star had been found, she did overhear Primrose at lunchtime telling Angel Seraphina that she was visiting the bunny four times a day and he was doing well. Angel Seraphina gave her another halo stamp for all her care and attention. Ella felt her heart twist. Now Primrose just needed one more to get her sapphire halo—just like Jess!

Remember what Poppy said, it's not a competition, Ella reminded herself firmly, as she walked away from Primrose and Angel Seraphina.

She found Poppy, Jess, and Tilly sitting in the sun, eating their lunches.

"What have you got there, Jess?" Ella asked, sitting down by Jess and seeing a large scrapbook beside her.

"Oh, it's nothing—just a project I've started," said Jess. "On glitter flowers."

"Have I missed something?" said Poppy in alarm. "Are we all supposed to be doing that? Is it homework?"

"No, don't worry." Jess grinned. "It was just something I wanted to do."

"Phew!" said Poppy.

"What sort of project?" Ella asked curiously.

"Well . . ." Jess hesitated, looking a little embarrassed. "I had this idea that if I put together all the things we know about glitter flowers, it might help us for next time—to stop us from running out again. Everyone seems to be very vague about when they flower and why. Angel Celestine just says that with enough care and love they'll eventually bloom—but she also says that in special conditions they can flower sooner. I thought if I wrote everything down it might help."

"It's a glittersome idea," said Tilly.

"Yeah," said Ella. She swallowed. It was a really good idea, and if Jess did it well it would be just the sort of thing to get her the last halo stamp she needed!

She instantly felt angry with herself. That wouldn't be why Jess was trying to do it. She wasn't like Primrose. She was just genuinely trying to be helpful. *But even so,* the little voice said, *she might get her sapphire halo and you've still got eight stamps left to go!*

Feeling uncomfortable, Ella got to her feet. "I'm going to go for a little walk," she said.

"Do you want some company?" Poppy asked.

Ella shook her head. She saw her friends glance at one another in concern. She knew they were starting to worry about why she was so subdued. "I'll catch you later!"

She headed off before they could come with her. She walked down toward the greenhouses and stopped by Star's shed. As usual it was locked. Ella sighed as she rattled the door. She would have loved to have cuddled the baby bunny. She sniffed suddenly. A strange, not very pleasant smell was coming from the slightly open window. What was it?

She fluttered her wings and flew up to the window. It was open just a crack. As she peered in, she let out a loud gasp. The hutch was filthy! Not only that, but the water bottle was nearly empty, and she could see the food bowl was bare too. Pitifully, the baby bunny scratched at the dirty straw in his cage. So much for Primrose checking on him four times a day!

Ella had to do something. She managed to get her hand in through the open window and undo the clasp, then she pushed the window open fully and climbed inside. Her white dress snagged on the wood, and as she pulled her way through, she got covered in dust, but she didn't care. She flew down to the floor and rushed to the hutch. "Oh, you poor thing," she said, looking at the sad little bunny. She opened the door and let him out, fetching him a bowl of food. While he hungrily started to eat, she cleaned all the dirty straw out, shoving it into an old bag and replacing it with fresh straw. Then she added hay to his living compartment and refilled his water bottle. The horrible musty smell in the air was going away now that the window was open fully.

"Oh, Star. Primrose hasn't been looking after you at all, has she?" she said, crouching down on the floor and getting even more dusty.

The little bunny looked at her anxiously. She gently picked him up and cuddled him to her. She could feel his tiny heart pitter-pattering, his fur was velvet soft against her cheek.

She stroked him over and over again until she felt him relax, and then she put him back in his hutch with a bowl of food. "Don't worry," she whispered to him. "I won't let Primrose get away with this!"

She felt furious. How could Primrose have forgotten to feed him? Why hadn't she been looking after him?

"I'll be back later to check on you, Star," she promised. "And I'll bring you some carrots. But first there's someone I need to talk to."

Ella flew back up to the window and wriggled out. It didn't take her long to find

Primrose. She was with Veronica, Olivia, and Susie on the other side of the grounds, playing angel volleyball. She caught sight of Ella and raised her eyebrows.

"Are you entering a dress-as-a-scarecrow competition? Or is it look-like-you've-been-dragged-through-a-bush-backward day?" She smirked.

Ella paid no attention. "How *could* you, Primrose?"

"How could I what?" Primrose said, but a guilty flush tinged her cheeks.

"I want a word with you," said Ella. "Away from here. Or I can say what I've got to say in front of everyone if you like?" she added.

"Er, no, all right, I'm coming," Primrose said hastily.

They stopped a little way off from the others.

"I went to see Star just now," Ella said.

"So?" Primrose looked defensive.

"His hutch was dirty, he didn't have any

food, and there was only a trickle of water in his water bottle!" Ella exclaimed furiously.

"All right, all right," said Primrose. "Keep your halo on!" She glanced at the others, who were looking at them curiously.

"You promised to look after him," Ella hissed. "You even got an extra halo stamp for it! I heard you telling Angel Seraphina all about how often you were visiting him. But you haven't been looking after him at all!"

Primrose looked sulky. "I've been to see him once."

"Once isn't enough—and you haven't cleaned his cage out at all!"

"So, what are you going to do about it?" A wary look crossed Primrose's face. "I suppose you're going to tell."

Ella hesitated. "No," she said, through gritted teeth. "I'm not." As much as she would have liked to, she didn't like people who tattled. "But I want the key to the shed. You're not to keep it locked anymore."

Primrose pulled out a small metal key from her pocket and handed it to her.

"And you'd better start looking after him properly," said Ella. "This is your last chance. If you don't care for him, I WILL do something about it."

"Oh, halos and wings, I'm so scared!" said Primrose, getting some of her usual confidence back now that she knew Ella wasn't going to tell. She flounced off toward the others who had started playing again without her. Ella stared after her. What was she going to do? She didn't want to tell Angel Seraphina, but what if Primrose didn't look after Star any better?

No problem, she thought, her fingers closing on the key. *I'll just look after him myself!*

CHAPTER 6

Angel Secrets

ELLA HEADED BACK TO STAR'S SHED.
As she got close to it, she saw Jess walking toward the greenhouses. "Jess!" she called,
keen to make up for being quiet earlier.

Jess smiled and waited for her. "Hi!" She
blinked as she saw the state of Ella's clothes.

"Goodness, what have you been doing?"

"Climbing through a window into Star's shed!" Ella quickly told Jess what had happened.

Jess was horrified. "But that's terrible!"

Ella nodded. "I know, but at least I found out, and I've got the key now so if Primrose doesn't look after him, I will."

"Shouldn't we tell Angel Seraphina that Primrose hasn't been taking care of him?" asked Jess.

"That would be tattling," Ella pointed out.

They looked at each other. Jess hesitated and then nodded. "I suppose."

"The important thing is that Star gets looked after properly from now on," said Ella. "Anyway, what are you doing here?" she said, seeing the sketchbook in her friend's hand. "Are you doing more of your project?"

"Yes. I thought I could draw one of the flowers," Jess said. "I tried drawing one from memory, but it was useless, and then I remembered what Angel Gabriella said in heavenly animals—about how sometimes it's easier to sketch from life, so I thought I'd come here and give it a try."

"Let's see the drawing you've done so far," Ella said.

Jess turned the pad around.

"It's ... um ... it's ..."

"Terrible." Jess sighed. "I know. I'm bad at drawing!"

Ella chewed her bottom

lip. The flower looked more like an oak tree! She felt the offer to help rise to her lips. She had helped Jess before with her drawings. *But that was before Jess only needed one more halo stamp to get her sapphire halo*, the little voice in her head said. Ella hesitated. She wanted to help, she really did. But . . . but . . .

"I'll go and have another try," said Jess cheerfully. "Maybe Angel Gabriella's right and I'll do a better drawing with the plant in front of me. See you later, Ella!"

She went on. Ella watched her. Her mouth opened and then shut again as she almost called her friend's name and then stopped herself. Jess went into the greenhouse.

Ella sucked in her breath. She should have offered to help. She knew she should.

It was jealousy again and she disliked herself for it. She was so lost in her thoughts that she didn't notice Angel Seraphina coming toward her.

"Penny for your thoughts." Angel Seraphina smiled.

"Oh, hello, Angel Seraphina," said Ella, jumping guiltily.

"Is everything okay, Ella?"

"Yes, everything's fine."

"It's just that you've seemed quieter than your usual self this week," said Angel Seraphina, her eyes meeting Ella's.

"Have I?" said Ella, startled that someone had noticed. "Oh. Well, I'm all right." She could hardly admit to a guardian angel—and a teacher at that—what she was feeling.

"Is it because Tilly has her sapphire halo?" Angel Seraphina said gently.

Ella stared. Could Angel Seraphina read her mind? "Oh, Angel Seraphina," she burst out, unable to hold it all in anymore. "I don't know why, but I can't stop feeling jealous. I can't bear it. I'm a useless angel. And a terrible friend, too!"

Angel Seraphina smiled. "Ella Brown, you are neither of those things."

"I am," said Ella miserably.

"No you're not." Angel Seraphina looked thoughtful. "You know, Ella, I knew an angel once who felt exactly the same way as you. Every time one of her friends went up a level before her, it ate her up inside. She didn't tell anyone, of course, but she hated herself for it."

"Really?" said Ella, surprised to hear that

another angel could possibly have felt the same way as her.

"Really," said Angel Seraphina. "And when her own best friend got a ruby halo before her—well, that was the very worst."

"And did that angel make it to the ruby stage herself?" asked Ella.

"She did indeed," said Angel Seraphina. She brushed down her dress and smiled. "She even made it to Guardian Angel level."

"You mean YOU?" said Ella, suddenly understanding what Angel Seraphina was trying to tell her.

"Yes, me." Angel Seraphina laughed. "Remember, I was a trainee guardian angel once too, and when I was at school I learned the important lesson that it's not how you *feel* inside that matters but how you *act* on those feelings."

Ella frowned. It definitely put a different take on things.

"I hope knowing that helps you, Ella," said Angel Seraphina. "Now I want to go and see how the glitter flowers are coming along. Do you want to come with me?"

Ella nodded. As she followed the teacher into the greenhouse, she realized that what Angel Seraphina had just said made perfect sense. You couldn't help the feelings you had— feelings just happened in your head. It was how you acted that made you good or bad.

They found Jess inside, sketching. "How's it going?" Ella asked, going over to her as Angel Seraphina walked around, inspecting the flowers with their tightly closed buds.

"Look!" Jess sighed and held up her pad. "Maybe if you can draw like Angel Gabriella then it's easier to draw from life, but not if you're as useless as me."

"Don't be silly, you're not that bad," said Ella. "First of all, you need to look at the proportions of the plant. At the moment, the leaves you've drawn are much too small and the stem too thick. Why don't you start again and I'll help you?"

They sat side by side, not even noticing when Angel Seraphina left the greenhouse, both engrossed in the picture. With Ella's help, Jess began to draw a plant that looked much more realistic. When the drawing was finally finished, she beamed.

"Oh, it looks perfect now, Ella," said Jess. "Thank you so much. When I hand my project in, I'll tell Angel Celestine how much you helped me."

"Don't be silly, Jess," Ella said. "This is your project. You did the drawing, I just gave you some advice."

"But you might get a halo stamp. . . ."

"I didn't do it because I wanted a halo stamp," Ella said. "I just did it for you."

Their eyes met. For a moment Ella thought the light in the greenhouse seemed to glow even more brightly. She blinked and everything was back to normal.

"Thank you for helping me," Jess said, standing up.

"I'm just glad I could," Ella said. They smiled at each other, and linking arms, they left the greenhouse together.

CHAPTER 7

Uncovered!

FOR THE REST OF THE DAY, ELLA WENT back and forth from the school to the shed to look after Star. There was neither sight nor sound of Primrose, but Ella didn't care about that. She was really enjoying looking after the little bunny herself. She felt so much happier since her talk with Angel Seraphina. Jess's project was almost finished and Ella was sure she would get a halo stamp for it when she handed it in, but suddenly she realized she felt okay about that. Of course she still wanted a sapphire halo herself, but Angel Seraphina had made her feel much better. She might not be one of the *first* to get a sapphire halo, but if she really tried to be good, she would fill her card and still get one. Just like Angel Seraphina had when she'd been younger.

Ella was much more her usual self with her friends that evening, and when Jess handed her project in to Angel Seraphina and got her final halo stamp, Ella celebrated with them all.

She slept really well that night, and in the morning she bounced out of bed, eager to go and see Star before classes started.

"Where are you off to?" Poppy asked as Ella pulled on her dress.

"To see Star."

"I'd like to see him too," said Poppy, who was still in bed. "I'll follow you down there when I'm dressed."

"Me too!" said both Tilly and Jess.

Ella smiled and set off. "See you all there!"

She flew toward the potting shed, humming to herself. As she opened the door, Star sat up and twitched his ears. He looked really happy to see her. "Hello, Star!" Ella opened the door

to the hutch, and he hopped out onto her lap. She cuddled him and then set to work cleaning it out. She had just finished and sat down to give the bunny another cuddle when there was a noise behind her that made her start.

"Oh, Angel Seraphina, it's only you," Ella said, smiling.

"Ella! I hadn't expected to find you here." Angel Seraphina looked surprised. "I saw the door open and thought Primrose must be in here. Is she around?"

"Er, I'm not sure. I haven't seen her," said Ella truthfully.

"Well, I'm sure she'll be here soon," said Angel Seraphina. "It looks like she's been looking after Star very well." She gave an approving look at the clean hutch.

"Here I am!" a breathless voice came from behind. It was Primrose. "Just doing my daily duty," she said, beaming. "Hello, Star, my sweetheart."

The little bunny shrank back, nuzzling farther into Ella's arms, his dark eyes wary.

Primrose ignored his alarm. "Star, it's me, come to Mommy," she crooned, reaching out. The bunny scrambled away, pushing against Ella's chest.

"Just wait a minute, let him settle down," Ella said, aware that Angel Seraphina was watching, a slightly puzzled frown on her face. Ella gave Primrose a pointed look, wanting to say, "let him get used to you first," but she didn't want to make it obvious that the bunny wasn't used to Primrose at all.

Impatiently, Primrose tried to pull him away from Ella. Star panicked and scrambled in her arms.

"Ow!" Primrose squealed, dropping him. "He scratched me!"

Star raced for the door and dashed out of the shed.

"Quick!" said Ella.

The angels hurried out of the shed and saw Star running in and out of the borders of the vegetable patch.

"Oh dear, we've got to catch him," said Angel Seraphina. "As he knows you best, you should go after him, Primrose."

"Me? Right . . . um . . ." Primrose swallowed as she went after the bunny. "Here, bunny. Nice bunny!" she cooed.

But every time Primrose got anywhere near him, Star ran away again. He started to look more and more anxious, darting this way and that with Primrose pursuing him. Ella couldn't bear it any longer. She pulled a carrot out of her pocket and headed over. She crouched down in a sitting position.

"Here, Star," she soothed. "Come to me."

The baby bunny's little nose sniffled at Ella's offering. Would it work? Would he go to her? Ella held her breath as the baby bunny took one tentative step in her direction.

"That's it," Ella crooned. "Easy does it."

One step . . . two . . . and Star was easily within Ella's reach.

"It's just a fluke!" Primrose said hastily. "I could have gotten him. I could have . . ."

"Be quiet, Primrose!" Angel Seraphina spoke sharply.

"There's a good boy." Ella smiled as Star drew closer and closer before he finally jumped into her arms for the waiting carrot. Ella stroked him and he nestled into her.

"Well done, Ella." Angel Seraphina smiled. Primrose looked like she was going to explode!

Once Star was settled back into his hutch with the door locked, Angel Seraphina turned to the two angels. "Is someone going to tell me exactly what is going on here? I want to know the truth."

Ella didn't say anything. Primrose remained silent too.

"Well, it's clear to me that Ella has been

helping you with Star," said Angel Seraphina. "Is that what's been going on?"

"Well, just a *little* bit," said Primrose.

"JUST A LITTLE BIT!" Angry voices came from behind. Ella looked around. Her friends—Poppy, Tilly, and Jess—were in the doorway and they looked furious. "Tell her, Ella."

"Well, I . . ." Ella didn't know what to say.

"Primrose didn't look after him properly at all," Poppy burst out. "Luckily, Ella realized that, and she cleaned his hutch and looked after him all day yesterday. She was going to look after him for the rest of the week without saying anything."

Tilly nodded. "She's the one who really cares about Star! That's why he likes her."

Angel Seraphina's eyes narrowed, and

for an angel, she looked pretty furious. "Is this true, Primrose? Is this what has been going on?"

"Well, um . . . maybe," Primrose mumbled, not able to meet Angel Seraphina's eyes.

The older angel looked angry. "That's it! I'm not impressed by this behavior. Not at all. Not only did you promise to look after Star, but you deceived me into thinking you were doing a good job of it too. You have neglected one of our heavenly animals and taken halo stamps for your efforts! I'm going to have to take all those stamps away, and another two for dishonesty."

Primrose looked aghast. "But, Angel—"

"No buts," said Angel Seraphina. "Ella, Primrose's stamps will go to you."

"To me?" said Ella, surprised.

"Yes, to you—not only for looking after Star, but for showing real angel qualities by not tattling and looking after him just to make him happy. There's a lot of good in you, you know, Ella Brown," she said. "An awful lot of good. Make sure you remember that."

Her friends gave a loud cheer and Ella looked embarrassed, but there wasn't time for that as, just at that moment, there was a loud shout from outside—right by the greenhouse. It was Angel Celestine!

"Over here!" she cried, running out the greenhouse door. "Come and see!"

The angels rushed over to the greenhouse and stepped inside. They couldn't see what

Angel Celestine was talking about at first. But then they couldn't believe their eyes. Not one, not two, not three, but ALL of the glitter flowers had burst into full sparkling bloom!

CHAPTER 8

Spring Picnic!

I JUST CAN'T UNDERSTAND IT," SAID Angel Celestine. "The only thing that would make the flowers bloom like this—other than patience and a whole lot of love and care—is if someone does a perfectly unselfish deed near the plants, but no one's been in to see them today."

"That is strange," said Angel Seraphina. "I wonder how it could have happened."

Jess gasped. "This deed? It has to be completely unselfish?"

"Completely and utterly," said Angel Celestine. "The person can't be hoping to gain from it in any way."

"Then I know who's responsible," Jess cried. "Ella, don't you see—it was YOU!"

"Me," said Ella, frowning. "But how?"

"Yesterday afternoon," Jess went on, her eyes shining. "We were in here and you did the most unselfish thing possible—you helped me with my glitter flower project, remember? And you did it knowing that it would get me the final stamp for my halo card and get me a sapphire halo—the very thing that you wanted yourself."

"I did?" said Ella, feeling embarrassed.

"Yes, you did," said Jess. She turned to Angel Seraphina. "I didn't tell anyone that

Ella had helped me with my project, but she did—she made all my illustrations work. I should have said. I didn't really earn that last halo stamp myself," she said.

"Oh, but you did," said Angel Seraphina. "The drawings were lovely, but I really awarded it to you for all the information you had gathered."

"Really?" Jess said shyly.

"Yes," said Archangel Grace. "And now that the flowers have bloomed there's no longer a glitter shortage, so the Spring Picnic can go ahead this weekend after all!"

"Hooray!" All of the angels let out a loud cheer, each giving Ella a thump on the back.

Ella turned to them and grinned. "I might

not have all my halo stamps this time, but I don't care! I know I'll get them in the end!"

The Spring Picnic was a huge success. Rugs were laid out covering the grass in Archangel Grace's private garden, and all sorts of delicious

angel foods were piled high—cloudberry cookies, honey sandwiches, towers of rainbow jelly, and big jugs of star fruit lemonade. There were even lollipops hanging on the trees. All of the angels were happy. Well, apart from Primrose. She was sitting on her own, sulking.

Veronica had become really good friends with Susie and Olivia and now they were playing tag together.

"Whoo-hoo," cried Poppy, as she slid down a massive rainbow slide in the middle of the garden. "Isn't this great!"

"The best!" Ella cried, as she swooped around with enormous pink and lilac butterflies that fluttered through the air.

"Oh, look, Ella, over there," cried Jess.

Ella looked over to the other side of the grass to where Jess was pointing, and there she saw a little familiar furry face with long ears and whiskers twitching. Star! They had released the baby bunny back onto the grounds the day before, but he kept coming back to check on them!

"I think he might be around for quite some time." Tilly grinned.

"Just like my friends!" said Ella, grinning as she linked arms with Poppy, who linked arms with Tilly, who linked arms with Jess. "Together, forever!"

MICHELLE MISRA
has written many stories for kids, including
the Magic Ballerina, Battle Champions, and
Wild Friends series. She lives in London,
England, with her family.